D0183898

DONALD **ANTRIM**

# THE
# HUNDRED
# BROTHERS

WITH AN INTRODUCTION

BY JONATHAN FRANZEN

GRANTA

*It is a pleasure to thank the MacDowell Colony and
the Corporation of Yaddo for their support.*

Granta Publications, 12 Addison Avenue, London W11 4QR

First published in Great Britain by Granta Books, 2013
Published by arrangement with Picador, Farrar, Straus and Giroux, New York
First published in the United States by Crown Publishers, Inc., a division of
Random House, Inc.

A CIP catalogue record for this book is available from the British Library.

1 3 5 7 9 10 8 6 4 2

ISBN 978 1 84708 653 2

Offset by M Rules

Printed and bound by CPI Group (UK) Ltd, Croydon, CR0 4YY

*For my father*

HARRY THOMAS ANTRIM

*and for his brother*

ROBERT ELDRIDGE ANTRIM (1940–1992)

*The Hundred Brothers* is possibly the strangest novel ever published by an American. Its author, Donald Antrim, is arguably more unlike any other living writer than any other living writer. And yet, paradoxically—in much the same way that the novel's narrator, Doug, is at once the most singular of his father's hundred sons and the one who most profoundly expresses the sorrows and desires and neuroses of the other ninety-nine—*The Hundred Brothers* is also the most representative of novels. It speaks like none of us for all of us.

Midway through his narrative, Doug spells out the fundamental fact that drives it: "I love my brothers and I hate their guts." The beauty of the novel is that Antrim has created a narrator who reproduces, in the reader, the same volatile mixture of feelings regarding the narrator himself: Doug is at once irresistibly lovable and unbearably frustrating. The genius of the novel is that it maps these contradictory feelings onto the archetypal figure of the scapegoat: the exemplary sufferer who recurs throughout human history, most notably in the person of Jesus of Nazareth, as an object of both love and homicidal rage, and who must be ritually killed in order for the rest of us to go on living with the contradictions in our lesser hearts.

In modern times, the role of the exemplary sufferer has come to be played by artists. Non-artists depend on and cherish artists for giving pleasing form to the central experiences of being human. At the same, artists are resented, sometimes even homicidally, for the dubiety of their moral character and for bringing to consciousness painful truths that non-artists prefer to remain unconscious of. Artists will drive you crazy, and *The Hundred Brothers* is a perfect instance of the work of art that seduces you with its beauty and power and then maddens you with its craziness. It's often hilarious, but there's always a dangerous edge to the hilarity. When, for example, Doug is describing the complicated seating chart for the dinner table at which he and ninety-eight of his brothers gather in a scene reminiscent of the Last Supper, he notes that his own name, unlike all the others, is written in "bright orange," and that he's "never been able to figure out the logic behind this." The orange writing recalls the fire that several brothers are building in the book's opening pages and the flames that illuminate the primitive ritual with which the book closes; the color targets Doug like a hunted animal. And the whole comedy of his situation—he simultaneously knows and resists knowing that he's his brothers' beloved and hated scapegoat—is encapsulated in his putative inability to "figure out the logic." Is the logic that Doug is the family's devoted genealogist, the former star quarterback of the family football team, the trustworthy listener to whom others turn with questions about God, and the brother who nurses his psychically and physically wounded brothers at the expense of his own needs? Or is it (as his narrative gradually and comically reveals) that Doug is a chronic liar and an unrepentant thief of his brothers' drugs and money, has a penchant for drinking too much and misbehaving, nurtures a bizarre fetish for his brothers' footwear, and once, as the quarterback in a crucial game, fumbled away the football in his own end zone? Or is it (as seems most likely) that Doug is the family artist, the outsider who is also the family's deepest insider, the brother who has taken it upon himself to annually assume the role of Corn King and perform "the nocturnal dance of death and the life that grows out of death"?

*The Hundred Brothers* speaks for all of us because we all inescapably feel ourselves to be the special center of our private worlds. It's a funny novel and a sad novel because this natural solipsism of ours is belied—rendered both ridiculous and tragic—by our ties of love and kinship to private worlds that we are necessarily not the center of.

At the level of technique, the book is a marvel: *has* to be a marvel, for, without supreme authorial control of scene and sentence and detail, it would collapse under the weight of its preposterous premise. In the opening sentence, Antrim manages to name and specify, through the magic of his commas and semicolons and dashes and parentheses, all ninety-nine of the brothers who have come together for drinks and dinner, bad masculine behavior, and avoidance of the work of giving their father's funeral ashes a proper burial. (This opening sentence also contains the book's first and last reference to a particular woman, Jane, who is responsible for the disappearance of the hundredth brother; it's as if, according to the novel's logic, the mere naming of a Significant Other is enough to exclude a brother from the narrative.) The story takes place entirely in the enormous library of the family's ancestral mansion, from the windows of which the campfires of homeless people can be seen in the "forlorn valley" outside the property's walls, and the action is confined to a single night, punctuated here and there by glimpses of the family's history of brother-on-brother cruelty and violence. (Doug's recollection of the childhood game of Kill the Man With the Ball, a game that embodies the love/hatred between siblings and prefigures their latter-day scapegoating ritual, is particularly inspired.) The incidents that occur on this single night are often farcical, often frustrating to Doug and to the reader, and always intensely vivid and specific. Taken together, they amount to a dextrous feat of choreography, in which Doug, the self-appointed Corn King, is the lead dancer who engages all the others as he makes his way around the library.

The novel is a feat of exclusion and inclusion, too. Left out of it are women (including, especially, the brother's mother or mothers), children, any reference to a particular place or year, and any realistic accounting of how there came to be so many brothers, how they all fit into a single house, and what their lives outside the house are like. Within these fantastical confines, however, can be found a remarkably complete catalog of the things that men do and feel among men. Football, fisticuffs, food fights, chess playing, bullying, gambling, hunting, drinking, pornography, pranking, philanthropy, power tools ("Doug, I need my belt-sander back," the brother Angus says in passing), homosexual cruising, anxieties about incontinence and penis size and middle-age weight gain: it's all there. The book also, despite its brevity, contains a deftly telescoped genealogy of human knowledge and experience, reaching from prehistory up through a very belated present day in which civilization seems to be teetering at the brink of collapse. Just as a vast collection of books and periodicals on every subject and from every era is housed in a single leaky and neglected library, so the totality of human archetypes ("the primeval aspects of the Self," in Doug's phrase) are gathered together in the single heroic, failing consciousness of the narrator.

When the brothers are all seated at the dinner table, one of them makes a call for better maintenance of the library: "As some of you may know, a slow drip, directly over Philosophy of Mind, has recently waterlogged and destroyed seventy to eighty percent of Cognitive Theory." As in some kind of nightmare of paralysis, however, the brothers are able only to notice the library's decay, not seriously combat it. Chandelier lights flicker, rainwater pours in, bats fly around, furniture is broken, food scraps are ground into once-valuable carpets. The entire novel is shadowed by the insight, or fear, or premonition, that postmodernity doesn't lead us forward but backward to the primitive: that our huge and hard-won sum of knowledge will ultimately prove useless and be lost. Already in the book's early pages, describing the eighteenth-century pornography that some of the married brothers are huddled over, Doug has intimations of this loss. "The Age of Enlightenment's inattention to hygiene is well documented," he remarks. "A certain syphilitic degeneracy lurks in these book-plate etchings of rheumy aristocrats making doggy love with their hats on." In the latter half of the novel, the intimations of decay become a drumbeat, culminating in the brilliant scene in which Doug himself ecstatically, with his urine, amid the shelved works of Liberal Theologians, Antiquaries, and Bibliographers, "hoses down, as they say, a few literary masterpieces." In the despair that grips Doug after this ecstatic moment, the dissolution of the library becomes increasingly indistinguishable from what's happening to him. The man has become the world, the world has become the man; the solipsism is complete; the narrative has gone fully mad.

The craziness of *The Hundred Brothers* derives from its willingness to embrace, even celebrate, the dark fact that an individual's life consists, finally, of an accelerating march toward decay and death. The novel is a Dionysian dream in which nothing, not even sanity, can escape the corrosive chaos of this circumstance; but its form is bravely Apollonian. It renders lonely solipsism universal and humane by way of rite and archetype and artistic excellence. What Nick Carraway says about his friend Jay Gatsby could also be said of the scapegoat Doug: he turns out all right at the end. The rest of us, his brothers and sisters, awaken from the harrowing dream refreshed and better able, as Doug says with equal parts of irony and hope, to "prosper and thrive."

# THE **HUNDRED BROTHERS**

**MY BROTHERS** Rob, Bob, Tom, Paul, Ralph, Phil, Noah, William, Nick, Dennis, Christopher, Frank, Simon, Saul, Jim, Henry, Seamus, Richard, Jeremy, Walter, Jonathan, James, Arthur, Rex, Bertram, Vaughan, Daniel, Russel, and Angus; and the triplets Herbert, Patrick, and Jeffrey; identical twins Michael and Abraham, Lawrence and Peter, Winston and Charles, Scott and Samuel; and Eric, Donovan, Roger, Lester, Larry, Clinton, Drake, Gregory, Leon, Kevin, and Jack—all born on the same day, the twenty-third of May, though at different hours in separate years—and the caustic graphomaniac, Sergio, whose scathing opinions appear with regularity in the front-of-book pages of the more conservative monthlies, not to mention on the liquid crystal screens that glow at night atop the radiant work stations of countless bleary-eyed computer bulletin-board subscribers (among whom our brother is known, affectionately, electronically, as Surge); and Albert, who is blind; and Siegfried, the sculptor in burning steel; and clinically depressed Anton, schizophrenic Irv, recovering addict Clayton; and Maxwell, the tropical botanist, who, since returning from the rain forest, has seemed a little screwed up somehow; and Jason, Joshua, and Jeremiah, each vaguely gloomy in his own "lost boy" way; and Eli, who spends solitary wakeful evenings in the tower, filling notebooks with drawings—the artist's multiple renderings for a larger work?—portraying the faces of his brothers, including Chuck, the prosecutor; Porter, the diarist; Andrew, the civil rights activist; Pierce, the designer of radically unbuildable buildings; Barry, the good doctor of medicine; Fielding, the documentary-film maker; Spencer, the spook with known ties to the State Department; Foster, the "new millennium" psychotherapist; Aaron, the horologist; Raymond, who flies his own plane; and George, the urban planner who, if you read the papers, you'll recall, distinguished himself, not so long ago, with that innovative program for revitalizing the decaying downtown area (as "an animate interactive diorama illustrating contemporary cultural and economic folkways"), only to shock and amaze everyone, absolutely everyone, by vanishing with a girl named Jane and an overnight bag packed with municipal funds in unmarked hundreds; and all the young fathers: Seth, Rod, Vidal, Bennet, Dutch, Brice, Allan, Clay, Vincent, Gustavus, and Joe; and Hiram, the eldest; Zachary, the Giant; Jacob, the polymath; Virgil, the compulsive whisperer; Milton, the channeler of spirits who speak across time; and the really bad womanizers: Stephen, Denzil, Forrest, Topper, Temple, Lewis, Mongo, Spooner, and Fish; and, of course, our celebrated "perfect" brother, Benedict, recipient of a medal of honor from the Academy of Sciences for work over twenty years in chemical transmission of "sexual language" in eleven types of social insects—all of us (except George, about whom there have been many rumors, rumors upon rumors: he's fled the vicinity, he's right here under our noses, he's using an alias or maybe several, he has a new face, that sort of thing)—all my ninety-eight, not counting George, brothers and I recently came together in the red library and resolved that the time had arrived, finally, to stop being blue, put the past behind us, share a light supper, and locate, if we could bear to, the missing urn full of the old fucker's ashes.

It was a wretched, pewter-colored day. The red library walls were haunted by shadows and light cast from a multitude of low-wattage reading lamps that haloed the tables on which they sat illuminating our laps as we flopped down on sofas and chairs overhung by English hunt prints and the heads of game animals, mounted, desolate, African, gazing out from rectangles of wall framed in wood shelves crowded with Victorian matched sets and works by obscure poets.

"I hate this room. It stinks of death," whispered Virgil, wedged beside me on a love seat. Virgil often felt, or he seemed to feel, to have felt, since his childhood, frightened and oppressed. It was impossible to say or do anything to make life less unpleasant for him. Nevertheless, we tried. "Lighten up," I told him. A line of our brothers scuffed past us in search of places to sit. The library was filling with male energy and low sounds of voices saying, "Hey, man, scoot over and make space." Soon it would be standing room only. The musty air would grow lush with our smells of sweat, shaving lotions, exhaled humid breaths. God help us. Already Virgil was hunched over on our shared cushiony seat, looking moist and claustrophobic with his head hovering between his knees, watery eyes scrutinizing the carpet. "Try reading a magazine," I suggested. Then, from a distant corner of the room—a crash, the jolting shatter of glass exploding, a lamp going down. This always happens when we crowd together in the red library: someone trips on a cord or backs into a three-legged table flaunting a bud vase, or hurls his body too heavily onto a chair, with the result that some *objet* or piece of heirloom furniture winds up noisily destroyed; it's alarming and inevitable and laughable. Today's mishap appeared to be the work of Max, who, clearly startled by the overturned light's impact, the noisy report of breaking china, stopped a moment to stare down at the lamp cord snarled around his ankle, the black electrical line snaking across the floor through porcelain strewn in brilliant white ruin near his shoes (the tiny conical lampshade having sprung free and gone flying, nearly knocking another lamp from another table), before looking up to gaze slowly here and there around the hushed room, then ask no one in particular, "Did I do that?"

Poor Maxwell. Ever since his return, last month, from a pharmacological botanical specimen–gathering expedition, he's been noticeably agitated, clumsy and distracted in the manner of one plagued by either fever or crisis. Apparently, something strange had happened in Costa Rica, and now Max was walking into things and breaking them, at a rate of about one electrical fixture, decorative serving dish, potted plant, or item of statuary every three days.

"What's wrong with him, do you think?" Virgil whispered barely audibly in my ear.

Together we watched Max kneel unsteadily down among the lamp shards. Siegfried and Stephen, both standing in Max's vicinity when the accident happened, came over and crouched beside their brother, helped him collect fragments, which they all painstakingly swept—their six outstretched, middle-aged hands raking and pawing the carpet for nuggets of porcelain and indiscernible, translucent bulb splinters—into a tidy pile. I was astounded by how fat Stephen had become. Just looking at him made me want a whiskey and soda. He scooped a quantity of particles into his soft hands and trotted off toward the fireplace, where, despite the fact that it was sufficiently warm in the room—and would become, what with the steady infiltration of more and more of our bodies, suffocatingly so—old Hiram was leaning on his walker, performing his customary patriarchal act of rudely supervising construction of yet another of his stupendous, raging fires.

"Ball those tight!" Hiram screeched at Donovan crumpling Sunday newspaper sections, lobbing these into the grate.

Hiram is ninety-three and universally despised for his many humiliating cruelties.

"Examine the flue!" he commanded Donovan, loudly enough for everyone in the family to overhear. And now Stephen quickly approached, head lowered and arms fully extended before him with hands cupped as if bearing something disagreeable, which, on arriving at the red-brick fireside, he flung away—a scatter of powder and detritus that clouded the hearth and the air around it with granular smog.

Immediately Hiram seized his walker by the handles and clattered backward, fleeing grime.

"Oh, my shoes, look at my shoes," he cried as a second cargo of glass and dust and, also, several large, knife-edged porcelain fragments, carried by Maxwell, made uneasy passage toward that end of the room. We all watched in horror as Max tacked around furniture and the extended legs of semireclining men. Everything was an obstacle, and Max seemed, with each wavering, anxious footfall, on the verge of keeling over. He vaulted an ottoman that appeared suddenly in his path. He kicked up rug corners. The rugs were ancient and valuable, tattered to a point near disintegration— but never mind, the real worry was that Max would do something grievous with that serrated porcelain he was brandishing in every direction. "Oh! Oh!" Hiram hollered as Max cleared the big Persian carpet, hit the hardwood, lost his balance completely, and flew into a run/slide/stagger across the floorboards toward him, toward Hiram clutching the walker with fists speckled brown by age. Max's arms thrashed, and it appeared he would crash into our eldest brother and cut off his head. But Hiram cowered down and used the waist-high, wraparound frame of the walker as a protective metal barricade. He lowered his head between bent elbows, thrust the walker before him, braced for collision—he'd once played sports! Now he showed admirable form, letting the walker absorb the initial impact, before recoiling from the main force of Max's oncoming midsection with a sideways feint-and-parry maneuver that would've been nice to watch on instant replay, it looked so effortless.

Max veered away. Hiram shook his fist—in anger it seemed, actually pain. He'd suffered an injury to the wrist, so easy to do at his advanced age. Now he clasped this brittle hand and crumpled over—automatically, self-protectively, in the manner of a man who's hammered his thumb. He shook out the hand and he made a face. Of course Barry came from wherever he was sitting to have a look. Barry's a caring physician and a loyal brother. He gives us all plenty of complimentary medical counseling, as well as phoned-in prescriptions for tetracycline or a refill of antidepressants. If the complaint requires a specialist's care, he'll offer a referral.

Barry flexed Hiram's wrist, massaged, tenderly, the hand and bony forearm. He swiveled the joint. "How's this? This? How about here? Okay? No? Hurt? Sorry." And so forth, as the old man grimaced.

Max in the meantime continued to weave. He still held that porcelain. What was he doing? Warding off an invisible enemy? No one dared approach him. It looked as if he might do serious damage after all.

"I wouldn't mind a hit of whatever he's on," whispered Virgil as the whirling botanist sheered back onto the Persian rug and into a crowd of twins. I couldn't help feeling, at that moment, a modest thrill. The twins invariably bunch together in a pack during social functions, refusing to mix with the rest of us, preferring to assert their own little club; and it's obnoxious. Suddenly, in rushed Max, a berserker in their midst, scattering three out of four identical twosomes. It was like something choreographed, Max dervishing armed and dangerous between Lawrence and Peter, on his left, and Scott and Samuel, to his right; and these two pairs at once deftly sidestepping—a shuffle of debonair panic followed by Max pirouetting to make straight for Winston and Charles tumbling backward onto chairs, raising hands to shield their matching terrorized faces crying, "Leave us alone! Leave us alone!"

That was when I noticed Max was wearing one of my favorite Italian ties. Isn't that the way in families. Someone's always rifling your closet.

"My tie!" I called across the room. The tie whipped and fluttered, as if blown in a wind.

But there was no actual breeze in here, only fear and turmoil, as guys of all ages got hastily up from their seats and retreated to form disorderly ranks before bookshelves and the recessed window casements between the shelves—a ring of brothers gazing in at Max with the same pitying, blankly frightened expressions worn by the taxidermized wildebeests and elk that loomed so dolefully overhead.

The library was about filled at this point. Only the last stragglers ranged up or down the lengthy hallways and stairwells that led to and from this or that distant household wing.

One by one we arrived. We were all present except George. Near the end of the line was Milton. I saw him coming through the library's main doorway.

Or not coming through. This entrance was clogged deep with Clinton, Rod, Bennet, Christopher, Leon, and many, many others, all intent on the spectacle at room's center: our brother stalking aimlessly, dangerously after nothing, pottery in his trembling hands.

Whispering Virgil told me, "I don't think he heard you. Look at him. This is very distressing. He needs help."

Maybe the thing to do would be for someone young and agile to storm out there and risk his body and just be a gladiator and tackle Max. Rush high, spear low, drive him hard to the carpet. Wham.

Quietly I said to Virgil, "Where's Zachary when you need him?"

"Fuck Zachary."

"Yeah, no shit. Fuck that guy."

"You know what I mean?"

"Yeah. Absolutely."

What *did* Virgil mean, exactly? And why was I agreeing with him? And *what,* by the way, was that low, whirring, humming sound coming from over by the fireplace?

The truth is, I like Zack a lot. Of course there were those times when we were kids, when he used stature and strength to gain advantage over smaller brothers. I'm thinking of the famous sickening instance when Zachary—who reached an imposing six feet seven and weighed in at two hundred and sixty virtually fat-free pounds *before* his seventeenth birthday, and who continued to grow, vertically and in girth, even after that—decided it'd be a gas to kneel on Virgil's chest, vigorously scour Virgil's naked stomach with a hairbrush, and yell out, in his ecstatic, hormone-enriched voice, "Red belly! Red belly!"

There were other, similar incidents, too, now that I come to dwell on it.

"Speak of the devil," growled Virgil.

Sure enough, it was the black-haired tormentor himself. Here he came plowing through a crowd at the opposite end of the room. Shorter men's heads bobbed around him. These heads got out of the way. Zachary's brothers let him pass. God, what hands that man had.

Would Zack notice Virgil and me snug on our tiny love seat? Or might he—and let's only hope!—overlook us and go after Max, whom he truly hated?

No such luck either way. Boys will be boys, even when they're men with heart conditions. This party, Zachary included, was decidedly into the show at center stage. Catcalls could be heard. "Go nuts, Maxwell!" someone shouted— prophetically?—as Max bumped a chair and almost fell.

"We're related to pigs," decreed Virgil.

Yes and no. *Pigs* is harsh. Virgil was evidently slipping into one of his moods. It is hardly my intention to take issue with another person's misery; nevertheless, I should say right now—at the outset of our evening together—that in this or any family certain moods and states of mind will be dominant and chronic to the extent that they are no longer perceivable as moods, but as routine personality traits, shared attributes—those supervening aspects of character that, because supervening, come to signify membership in the family circle. The collective persona of this family could reasonably be described as frantic, romantic, lethargic, sarcastic, fearful, frustrated, tipsy, pugnacious, unchaste, heartless, dog-eat-dog, borderline narcissistic, nervously narrow-minded, and more or less resigned to despair although occasionally festive when inebriated. This can be problematic. The fact that we all abide depression does not lessen the pain of the lonely sufferer lost among raucous celebrants. When dealing with Virgil, I always assume the worst. "Don't make me ask Barry to give you a shot," I told him, and he lowered his head in his hands and groaned. As usual, I had taken the wrong course.

"I'm sorry, Virgil. I didn't mean that."

"Yes, you did. You pretend you're my ally, but you're the same as all the rest."

"No one is going to give you a shot."

"Why do you have to say something like that? You know how that makes me feel."

"I said I was sorry. I'll say it again. I'm sorry. It was a stupid and insensitive thing to say. I shouldn't've. Here"—putting my arm gently around his shoulders, giving a supportive, brotherly squeeze—"it's okay, it's okay. Calm down. Everything will be all right."

"I don't want to be that way anymore, Doug. I don't want to be the way I was."

"You won't."

"Promise?"

"Yes."

He hunched over, head in hands. Virgil's body shivered, and he sounded as if he might be crying. "I want to die," he said.

"We're all going to die soon enough, Virgil. There's no reason to wish for death."

At which point, and, as if on cue, Max did tumble to the floor. It was beautiful and balletic: Maxwell's body arcing downward in face-forward descent with arms extended overhead, hands outstretched and still holding the pieces of the heirloom lamp he'd smashed at the outset of our gathering in this big red room—holding these pieces aloft and ablaze in the reflective incandescence of reading lamps constelled on tables everywhere: our homey little indoor Milky Way of 40-watt bulbs lighting up the library's run-down leather furniture and desiccated animal heads and innumerable, dusty, unread books; and our faces, all our faces lit amber and watching Maxwell's long body plunge belly flopping toward moth-eaten carpet bunched in folds set to snare and entangle the botanist's drunken feet.

"The God is among us!" the falling man shouted out on his way down.

Then thump.

"Ouch!" someone nearby exclaimed, reflexively, as Max made contact. His thud accompanied by porcelain launched clattering across the floor. Porcelain bursting into smaller fragments. Skidding under chairs.

"Good Lord," said a voice.

"Doctor!" called another.

And from far away in the rear of the mob blocking the door, the high voice of dear, sweet Milton, the channeler, asking anyone and everyone, "What happened?"

The bottleneck in the doorway broke up. A half dozen fellows cleared into the room. Curious others followed. More filed in to sit or stand gawking at Max.

"He freaked out," Siegfried told Milton. In Siegfried's callused hands were further remains of the busted lamp. Now the sculptor peered warily down at this glass he carried—as if it might somehow be hazardous, might hold the power to bring him harm. He explained to Milton, "Max tripped on a light cord and broke this light, no big deal, right, and Stephen and I were helping clear the mess. All of a sudden Max takes off chasing after people."

"He tried to assassinate me!" wailed Hiram from over by the fireplace. Hiram heaved up an arm. He displayed his swollen hand. His face showed pain.

"Us, too!" chorused twins Winston and Charles in unison from their sanctuary behind a leather sofa.

By this time Barry'd made it to Max's side and was kneeling in doctorly fashion, attending to the toppled man.

Max lay flat on his stomach, not moving at all. Barry reached out to examine him; he pressed for heart's cadence above Max's collar. There was a hush. Shuffling of feet. A cough. A chair cushion sighed beneath somebody's shifting. Silence, and in the silence that vaguely familiar, low whirring sound that had seemed to come, moments earlier, from the vicinity of the fireplace. What could it be. Oh, of course. It was Fielding with his eight-millimeter home-movie camera. He was zooming in, adjusting the focus, finding the light, getting everything on film.

"Give me a hand here, someone," Barry said without looking up at anyone in particular.

Nobody moved. Eyes met eyes as the camera's motor softly, metallically purred. The camera panned across floor and Max's still back; its bluish lens pulled in tight over pair after pair of shoes nestled beneath cuffed and uncuffed trousers worn by men standing close. Fielding's camera's gaze passed right up those trouser fronts, up over the pleats and the plackets covering zippered or buttoned closures, up to check out the pockets stuffed with hands rammed down into them, playing absently with gum wrappers and balled-up money and keys and lint and change and receipts from purchases.

Playing, as well, with genitals. Our ninety-nine, not counting George's, sets of underwear-enshrouded nuts.

"Put that goddamned thing down," some brother or other told Fielding, who was at that instant raising his camera to take in, in steady lateral progression, our faces in sequence.

It was one of our everyday eternal moments of collective, mute indecision—in this instance over who would do what, if anything, to help Barry help Max.

A little clique in front seemed to wake up. Three came forward and positioned themselves around Maxwell. Following the doctor's instructions—"It doesn't appear that anything is broken. I want to try to get him turned over. Milton, put your hand under Max's knees. Siegfried, watch his arms. Christopher, you hold his feet. I've got the head. Okay, we're going to lift and roll, gently, on three. To the right. Careful. One, two, *three*"—they grunted and shifted the prone man from his stomach to his back.

In other parts of the library, other things were taking place. It is easily possible, in a room such as this, for many activities to take place simultaneously, without significant disturbance to the informal reader or browser paging through baroque musical scores or the occasional dated literary, scientific, or heraldic tract pried from the heart of an uncataloged loose stack. I mention our vast heraldic holdings because they are of special interest, lately, to me. Genealogy—and by genealogy I mean more than mere sketching and labeling of "family tree" diagrams; rather, the deep investigation into bloodline and blood's congenital inheritances, particularly in connection with insane monarchs—has become a primary avocation of mine. I'm not crazy. But I do have the blood of an insane monarch running through my veins. We all do. I wanted to know what, if anything, this might portend. So

I've been spending nights doing layman research into intrafamilial sociobiological matters, spreading decomposing documents on the oak table beneath the rose window that
would look down—if you could only see through those
darkly stained indigo panes—onto cobbled footpaths and
stone bridges here and there traversing grassy plots, onto the
several interconnected, smelly, evaporating ponds encircled
with old trees that were lush once though never tall, bowed
lower still by their years and all but leafless on their way to
dying, our former topiary garden. So much here suffers de-
cline. The red library everywhere shows the years since anybody bothered picking up a putty knife. Browning paint
and yellow plaster molts like a skin from the cross-vaulted
ceiling. Of twenty chandeliers pendent from twenty golden
ropes, only a few manage any real light. The effect, when
looking up, late on a winter day as evening wanes to black,
is unsettling: a Piranesian study of listless candelabra teth-
ered beneath obscurely lit, cracked domes that, depending
on illumination's intensity and the various reaches of shadows flung every direction by the intersecting lattices of the
vaults, appear alternately higher or lower, more ruinously
beautiful or hideously spectral than they actually, probably,
are—an entire grim structure in want of some kind of repair before it simply breaks apart and descends, faulty light
fixtures and all raining down on our heads. Or so it would
seem to the anxious reader obsessed with death. And on the
subject of heads! From where I sat, squeezed into the love
seat beside disconsolate Virgil, I was able to gaze more or

less eye to eye at no fewer than one dozen lifeless mammals, wall-mounted, across the way, on plaques (the lone exception in this grouping, a reindeer that has had eyes gouged out, leaving wounds)—each among them wearing humiliation in one guise or another: lacerated ears poking through matted gray mane, chipped antlers or horns and the teeth either missing by the mouthful or cracked off blackly at their roots, general depilation under coatings of dust. Poor squandered animals. My heart goes out to them. Their faces seem to scream out final terror. What a crummy way to spend the afterlife, tacked up in a room full of men falling down or shouting obscenities at each other while getting their rocks off to eighteenth-century French and English pornographic works on paper—a main particular of interest among our special collections here, especially (Predictably? Understandably?) to the younger married fellows, who act as if the stuff doesn't affect them in the least, yet who are invariably, whenever we gather socially, the first to make tracks to the mahogany and glass cabinet where it is stored. Whom did they think they were fooling anyway? There they were, those horny bastards over in their corner, Seth and Vidal and Gustavus and Clay, all the usual snickering crowd passing pages and quietly boasting, "I'd do her"—even while their brother the rainforest plant scientist lay semicataleptic, drooling, incontinent, out of his mind not more than twenty feet away. Don't get me wrong. I do not intend prudery. I like a good erotic illustration, and these are very artfully made pictures, beautiful in the way Hogarth's Gin Lane engravings are

beautiful, which is to say flamboyantly grotesque and therefore fantastically curious to the furtive voyeur—well, I enjoy
a good erotic image as much as the next person. But these
dressing-room scenes of rickety-legged libertines putting lean
penises into corpulent mistresses doubled over atop banister
railings or the gilt backs of chairs (the women's skirts parted
behind to reveal poorly delineated genitals, a fleeting glimpse
of thigh)—these dressing-room and scullery and opera-box
tableaux are far more disturbing (in what they have to say
about private life, public health, and the history of European
sexual fashion and taste) than erotic. The Age of Enlightenment's inattention to hygiene is well documented. A certain
syphilitic degeneracy lurks in these bookplate etchings of
rheumy aristocrats making doggy love with their hats on.
Even the paper on which they are reproduced abides in a condition of yellowing decrepitude that only worsens the seeming
pallor, the intrinsic sickliness of the figures. Seth, Vidal, Gustavus, and Clay do not appear to be bothered by this death
imagery, maybe because they're married and feel they'll live
forever through progeny. It's that old bloodline problem.
There's no getting away from the drive to procreation. Celi-
bacy would lead straight to boredom and the aimless waiting
that is a precondition of renewed passion for life. What is this
red library if not an oppressively furnished waiting room
where grown men shift uneasily from foot to foot while
launching small harangues about work or sex or their archaic
interpersonal grievances, still viable, from our hundred over-

lapping childhoods? Indeed. Some manner of clamorousness was in progress over by the towering shelves where the *National Geographic*s are stacked—it was Foster getting heated up about his favorite topic, the imperiled cosmos. We've all had to sit through Foster's impromptu rants about mankind's fate. Andrew was his unlucky prey this evening.

"I'm very serious about these evolving dangers, little brother," Foster cautioned Andrew. He had Andrew pushed against a magazine rack. Insistence is crucial to Foster's conversational style. Tonight he was worked up. He leaned forward, glared directly into Andrew's face, and proclaimed, "The earth changes are coming. Everything points toward massive geophysiological change. I've been saying this for years and I'll say it again. Oceans rising! Plants and mammals becoming extinct! Inner cities dying and genetic calamities of every order sauntering around like it's Sunday in the park!"

"What are you talking about, Foster?"

"I'm talking about the coming wave of brand-new cancers spreading everywhere like the common cold during the global red tide of the immediate futures."

"Future*s*?"

"Sure. The future is the aggregate of all tenable futures of individual selves," exclaimed Foster, as if to a child. Then he declared, "You know, Andrew, I really admire the work you do with the homeless."

"What do you mean?"

"Just that."

Now in the red library the light was diminishing; evening was falling and the winter sky outside looked ashen against the clear windowpanes overlooking the east. What time was it anyway? That glum hour before moonlit night. The cocktail hour. Why wasn't there a fire in the hearth? Where was Spooner? Spooner always carried hooch.

"After all, aren't we *all* indigent, in a metaphysical way?" Foster was saying to Andrew, intensely. Foster's face was red and his eyes burned with belief in something larger than himself. Our Foster has at one time or another shrilly publicized the most amazing things: synchronicity, interspecial telepathy (animals read our minds), seraphic intervention (angels help us succeed in life), morphic resonance (every member of a genetically interrelated family group, no matter how widely dispersed or apparently dissimilar, will immediately comprehend or embody the changed attributes and learned abilities of one individual), Possible World Theory, Chinese astrology, and assorted ancient divinations of planetary transformation in the years after the millennium. If Foster has his way, we'll all be abandoning our depressions in favor of united, heartfelt crusading for wide-scale spiritual reform. In this respect—this grave interest in working for causes—grandiose Foster is not unlike his more pragmatic brother Andrew, who often takes time out during family functions to pass the hat for donations to aid the residents of the flourishing tent city that has sprung up, virtually overnight it seems, in the untilled meadow beyond the garden gate, just outside our walls.

I always give Andrew whatever silver comes from my pockets. You can see their fires out there, late at night.

"Is it cold in here or is it me?" whispered Virgil.

"There is definitely a draft," I told him. His body, squeezed close beside mine on our tasseled and embroidered love seat, felt damply warm; his cheeks and white forehead wore that pasty sheen that accompanies Virgil's recurrent nighttime fevers. "Do you want my sweater?"

"No."

"Are you feeling all right?"

"Once Hiram gets the fire going I'll be fine."

"Sure?"

"Positive."

"Let me know."

"Kind of you. Thanks."

We turned our gazes then to take in the scene around Maxwell. The fallen man was laid out on his back and surrounded by feet. Maxwell wasn't moving. His clothes were a mess. At his head knelt Barry. Other men peered from behind Barry, and behind these were more looking down with eyes fixed on Max's face and the doctor's hands. Barry seemed to be reaching inside Maxwell's mouth. Yes, Barry did have a hand in Maxwell's mouth, fishing around there. Then he removed the hand. He took a vast inspiration of breath. Barry pinched Maxwell's nose shut between fingers and thumb, lowered his own mouth to Maxwell's, and blew a series of puffs.

"This is serious," someone said. And it was as if the saying of this made everything true—our dear brother's life in danger and all of us lollygagging ineptly on the furniture (all except Barry hunkered low over Maxwell's head, blowing, blowing). It was like that time when Vincent was five and fell off the roof and only Raymond and Nick were around playing in the yard, and they were too young to grasp the severity, so Vince dragged himself bleeding across the gravel and up the steps into the front hall where he passed out in a lagoon of his little boy's blood. No one particularly knew what to do then, either. Thank God for Barry. Fortunately, Maxwell was not bleeding. There did appear to be a twig of something green and leafy sticking out from the breast pocket of Maxwell's blazer.

And quietly came the sound of Virgil's voice, the humid feeling of his breath tickling my ear, as he brought his face close to mine and complained vehemently, "Fuck. It's Chuck's dogs."

It was the truth. Here dogs came, whipping through the library's tall eastern doorway, claws viciously scraping hardwood, one fleet Doberman and one shedding English sheepdog, Gunner and Rolfe, off the leash as usual and tearing obnoxiously for Maxwell's body as if it were a toy for them to pounce on and lick.

"Whoa!" cried Henry.

"Careful!" hollered Arthur.

"Dogs!" yelled James.

"Look out!" warned Simon.

Then both dogs were atop him. Paws flailing Max. Walking on Max's stomach. Tongues out.

"Grab its leg!"

"Get your hand around the mouth!"

"The other way!"

"Pull them off his head!"

Then the sound of Foster, piercing and distinct: "Leave them alone! They *know*! They're trying to *help*! They want to *revive* him! It's what dogs *do*!" shouted the animal telepathist.

"Screw that," someone said as, from the direction of the door, the voice of the dogs' owner, Chuck, a prosecutor for the county and just now following the dogs into the room, commanded, with authority:

"Sit."

Obediently dogs climbed down from man and came to rest on either side of inert Max. There they stood, two intent and furry guardians watching over his form. Discreetly the dogs peered up at faces glaring down at them and at Maxwell's face and hair lacquered in dog spit. The botanist's shirt and my Italian silk tie were gummy with wetness from these dogs' panting and drooling. Barry'd been knocked back by their lunges and now grumbled a complaint while righting himself. Gunner in his studded collar bared teeth and growled.

Luckily, this animal's master approached bearing leashes

and a pocket stuffed with treats. In that imperturbable, crooning voice dog owners adopt when addressing misbehaving pets, Chuck called, "Easy there, Gunner boy, easy. Gunner, good boy, good dog, easy Gunner-gun, good dog."

The Doberman became sullen. Chuck produced the snacks. He tossed these through the air toward his dogs' mouths. Sheepdog and Doberman swung heads to make ace catches without any movement away from Max's side.

That sheepdog is a sweetheart, but everyone fears the other, thanks to its breed.

Of course all this incited reproaches from Barry, who declared, "I'm trying to revive your brother. Why don't you control these animals. Especially *that* one," glowering at the Doberman.

Chuck rose to the dog's defense. "Gunner never hurt anyone. These are the sweetest creatures on God's earth. Leave Gunner alone."

"Here, boy," Chuck said to his Gunner, dispensing another treat into the mouth of the black-and-cinnamon purebred. Gunner's eyes shone maniacally. He was all pent up. As were we all in that long moment while the sun went down outside and lamp-thrown shadows lengthened across the darkening walls of the enormous red room.

Dogs chewed. Barry felt around for intimations of Maxwell's vital signs. Siegfried, Christopher, and Milton stood awaiting doctor's orders to assist if need be. Rolfe, the woolly sheepdog, sniffed, affably, Maxwell's clothing. No one seemed to notice Rolfe sniffing the mysterious green branch coming out of Max's breast pocket. A stick! Rolfe gathered leafy stick into sopping mouth and off he trotted with it. Gunner eyed this. Nearby, someone sneezed. A reaction to dogs? It is impossible to keep track of who is allergic to what around here. All of us get skin rashes, and someone is always sneezing, and someone else always has a cough or the flu, and someone else is forever about to throw up. How much can you truly know about other people's afflictions?

"Would someone please bring me my bag?" Barry asked in his usual authoritarian manner—as if speaking to an orderly.

The bag was over by the fireplace. Hiram was closest to it. Christopher fetched it.

"Oh, God, please don't let him give Max a shot," whispered overwrought Virgil, who buried his head in his hands and absolutely would not look when Christopher brought the bag to Barry, who opened it up and extracted latex surgical gloves, cotton, various utensils. Gunner, being a dog, could not resist investigating with his nose. "Get the dog away," said Barry, hoisting a small vial containing what turned out to be an opiate antagonist administered to counteract respiratory depression induced by narcotic overdose. How did a general practitioner happen to stock a bottle of something like this in his doctor's kit? The answer is simple and pitiful. Over the years, Barry has had to bring many of us—including Virgil here—down from bad trips.

Max's face was ashen. His brothers in a ring peered down at his staring eyes. "Why's his tongue green?" asked Siegfried, still clutching porcelain fragments. Fielding with his eight-millimeter circled the scene, trying different angles. Finally Chuck dragged Gunner away by the collar and leashed him to an art nouveau armchair; this space vacated by the dog allowed Fielding a clear alley to shoot through. "Uh, can someone move that coffee table a tad to the left? *My* left. Back a little. Watch the edge of the carpet. Perfect. Don't anybody move, okay?" Fielding cautioned his brothers. Meanwhile Chuck humored his animal. "Sorry, buddy, I have to tie you up," Chuck said. The Doberman, restrained, started barking. The dog's loud noise caused Virgil to look up surprised. At that moment Barry did the things doctors do with vial and syringe, the flourish of bottle and needle as the liquid is drawn into the hypodermic payload.

"Oh, no," whispered Virgil.

"Try not to let it bother you," I said to him.

"I can't help it, Doug. I see one of those things and everything starts turning black and I feel like I'm being strangled."

I put my arm around him, and he tried to move away, to rise from the love seat, but he couldn't because we were pressed together too tightly on it. So I held him closer, and after a restless moment he ceased moving and sat quietly beside me, though his eyes worked left then right, left then right, looking anywhere but directly ahead and never settling on Barry and Maxwell. I recognized this state as a paranoid regression of sorts: Virgil's bodily quiescence, the rigid and insistent placidity mediated by acute cerebral hypervigilance.

It was as if forbidding thoughts lay perilously in wait, unwelcome feelings that even simple physical movements might shake free and liberate. As I have already pointed out, Virgil's childhood years were not cheery. He suffered ailments, and several times came close to death. He was picked on mercilessly.

I grabbed Virgil's arm and pulled him close to me as, from room's center, the voice of Barry commanded, "Push Max's sleeve up, someone."

Christopher did this, and Barry plunged the needle in Maxwell's arm.

"There," Barry said when the job was done. Fielding behind his camera added, "That's a wrap."

Inappropriate remarks like the above are what make us hate Fielding and his pointless movies of whatever sorrow we happen to be going through. Why even dignify him with a response? Barry explained, "Max's tongue is green from leaves he's been chewing. See these flecks?" He stuck a rubber-gloved finger in Maxwell's mouth and swabbed one out as Fielding started his camera again and leaned in for an extreme close-up. "Some kind of botanical psychoactive he must've picked up in the jungle. Probably a datura. It's anybody's guess how long Max has been hallucinating. Several hours, possibly longer. Did anyone happen to see Max earlier in the day? No? Heart rate is down and respiration is impressively low. The pupils are contracted and exhibit minimal sensitivity to light. I've given him Narcan, intramuscularly, to counteract the narcotic. What is it with you guys and your drugs? Can someone *please* get the *dog* to be *quiet*?"

Amazingly, for without pressure from its owner, Gunner did fall silent. I must presume under the circumstances that the dearness of life, the value of it, its perceived worth—though neither *value* nor *worth* describe, fittingly, the crushing weight, for friends and relations at least, that a life has when threatened with its own ending—I must, under these grim circumstances (the doctor's frustration with the patient's condition; the dog's shutting up; the young husbands' soberly putting away their antiquated smut), presume that this so-called, by me, dearness of life can, in fact, be read in the demeanor and the attitude, the conscious or unconscious *deportment* of the average onlooker waiting a seeming eternity for the good or the bad news—even if the onlooker is, alas, a dog. I say this because of the way we all took, from Gunner's sudden cessation of baying, our own cues to make like Max and *stop breathing* (if such were possible!—all hundred of us, not counting George, gathered around and taking in, holding in, simultaneously, those brisk little audible inhalations that indicate distress, curiosity, skepticism, hope)—to make like Max and stop breathing, and to consider, sympathetically (Didn't we all feel a bit giddy and faint-headed ourselves, sitting or standing or kneeling there deliberately without oxygen?), how Max, if he *had* any feeling, must've felt in that moment while his lungs strained to get going—how lonely and how cold—and, also, how much we really did love him, would love his memory if he passed away from us. Even black-haired, towering Zachary, whose emotional life is too often characterized by violent, jocular aggression toward the weak and humble, seemed subdued, genuinely concerned over Maxwell's welfare, or, at any rate, sensitive to the mood of concern suffusing the room. Zachary knew better than to give anybody an arm burn now. Back at a distance he stood, fists in pockets, head bent forward. (What size could Zachary's shoes be? Do they make a fifteen? I'd like to know.) And Hiram, over by the fireplace, seemed to have forgotten, for the time being, the fire he had earlier undertaken to engineer. Blankly he peered over his walker. His wrist was swollen hugely but he was paying no mind. At his side his helper, Donovan, clutched, in delicate pink hands, a wad of incompletely crumpled Sunday newspaper. Donovan remained extremely still, because to move at all would mean possibly rustling that paper, a rudeness for sure in light of the suspense we all felt as Barry leaned over to massage Maxwell's chest.

Fielding's camera whined. The married guys watched it all from over by the porno cabinet; they, like Zachary, had their hands stuffed deep in their pockets, and one (Clay) showed, beneath worsted trousers, a boner.

It is true that we have all seen one another undressed at one time or another, and the range of our sizes is, I can report, exactly as you might suspect. What can be said about a hundred penises of all ages? Clay had a pocketed hand wrapped around his. Gently, absently, through the pocket's cozy inner lining, Clay kept himself hard.

"Doug, I think I need some air," Virgil whispered, very quietly even for Virgil. He was watching the floor. Needle fear had made him sweaty.

"Right. Good idea," whispering back in that hush of the library fraught with expectancy and tension, tugging on his arm. "Come on. I'll help you."

"I'm all right. Let go of my arm," Virgil insisted.

"I don't mind. You stand up and I'll help. We'll slip out to the gazebo and relax on a bench and watch the homeless people light their campfires in the meadow."

"Doug, you're hurting my arm. Please! I don't want to go to the gazebo."

A scattering of brothers swiveled heads to frown in our direction. One of these—it was Roger in his cowboy boots—waved. Neither Virgil (hunched uneasily over, palms clammy on knees) nor I (hands securely affixed to Virgil's forearm) dared wave back. If you show Roger indication of receptivity to him, he'll come over.

To Virgil I said, "You're making a spectacle."

"I'm sorry."

"If I let go of your arm, will you pull yourself together and behave?"

"Yes."

"I don't want you running off. All right? I don't want to have to come hunting for you."

Gloominess from Virgil. Dead animals gazed down. Among the men gathered around Maxwell, a solemn, ethnomedical colloquium was in progress. Certain words— "rapture," "zombie," "potential blindness"—and longer phrases—"extensive psychomotor damage" and "Indigenous peoples along the lower Amazon use these substances in spirit rituals" and "Actually, in some cases, *humans*"—escaped, now and then, to rise up and echo dully against the bleak vaults above our heads. Finally from out of this ad hoc conference there came a wail, loud at first and growing louder like some animal's sound. Every brother turned. The Doberman, hearing the sound, bounded from his place leashed to the armchair and made his own racket tugging things over. No one paid any attention to this. The wail rang out. It was coming from Max. Brothers closest to the sound did not know whether to approach or retreat as, first, Max's hands, then his feet, next arms, and at last Maxwell's legs began to tremble and to flail, all extremities storming the air near Milton and Siegfried and our young Christopher. Backward these three now fled. There was no holding their brother. Violently Max beat the air. Only Barry persisted—dutifully—in trying to comfort Maxwell's sputtering head in his lap. "A tongue depressor! Hurry! In my valise!" cried the MD, but it was too late for this as Maxwell's open hand swung furiously upward to slap Barry's face and knock eyeglasses flying and the doctor himself tumbling backward against a table leg that stove him in the head. "Uhf," Barry said. Then Fielding's camera's battery-powered spotlight bleached everything white, as Fielding climbed more or less aboard Max, shot down on the pharmacobotanist, took blows in the process. Fielding's commitment to his craft was inspiring. Nevertheless, there was something garish about this scene. The documentary-film maker's art is not only voyeuristic (we are, after all, meddlers in one another's lives), but opportunistic—our poor Max suffering epiphanies on the rug and his own brother satisfied to hover above him and film it! Maxwell punched deliriously at nothing we could know. The noise rising from him was magnificent. It was a sound you might imagine coming out of a man being opened with a knife. It hurt to hear it. Virgil, hearing it, got that terrorized look he gets, eyes showing white, not a good sign, and I thought it'd likely be advantageous under these circumstances to go ahead and squire him around back for some air, so said to him, "Let's go, Virgil." Unfortunately leaving became immediately unfeasible. Max's long scream, nearing its end, turned articulate. From the Persian carpet at the heart of the room, Maxwell, breathless and bloodlessly pale beneath Fielding's camera shining down on him in his distress, cried, "Doug! Doug!"

And was quiet again.

Hands twitched a little. Chest rose and fell. One foot kicked its mate.

For a moment no one seemed ready to make a move. Men near Max watched him. A few raised eyebrows, nodded my way; whispers were passed. Barry clutched his head—the doctor seemed disoriented. Kevin in a low voice said, "Here you go, Barry," and handed Barry his glasses, which had landed unharmed over by General Non-fiction C–E.

And I could hear other sounds in the room. Max's hard breaths, and the creaking made by old floorboards underfoot as, one after another, brothers shuffled to left or right, little by little opening a path between the love seat and the place where Max lay bathed in light and sweat.

Fielding did not miss a beat. He whirled his camera to shoot up this impromptu corridor of many brothers fanning backward to make way for—for what? Virgil raised hands to shield eyes from the high-wattage brightness suddenly pouring in on us. For my part, I hate appearing in Fielding's motion pictures, no matter the occasion. There always comes a time when we have to sit around on folding chairs and watch the things, and someone always has to pop corn, and Fielding always has to solicit comments on the effectiveness of his work, and this is not enjoyable; it's rude.

Now Fielding was motioning to us—to *me,* actually—with his free hand, making a directorial "steady now, walk toward the camera" gesture.

"Shall we?" I said to Virgil.

"You go. Max wants you."

"I'd appreciate it if you came with me."

"Do I have to?"

"No. It's up to you. I'm inviting you to join me, if you'd care to."

"What do you think he meant when he said, 'The God is within us'?"

"He said, 'The God is *among* us.'"

"'Among us'?"

"I believe that's what Max said. We'll have to ask him, won't we? Let's find out how Max is feeling, then we'll sit somewhere quiet."

"Can we get something to drink?" Virgil asked.

"You bet."

"Because I'm very thirsty, Doug."

Getting up from the love seat was difficult. Virgil had trouble. It was a matter of leverage. The love seat was low and our knees were high. We made a false start in which Virgil dug his fist into my ribs as I tried pushing until something hurt in my back and Virgil foundered. Light from Fielding's handheld camera flashed around us; the light threw colossal human shadows, the shadows of brothers, onto far walls. Larry stepped directly into the camera's sights; his enlarged likeness spanned shelves and windows almost to molding level. Daniel's likeness flickered hugely across the room, a monster en route to the door where, at that moment, Albert entered, as the blind will, tapping, with his retractable cane, a route among the furniture legs. "Good evening, gentlemen," Albert said without moving his head. Fielding rotated the camera to follow Daniel steering Albert carefully past Max, and toward his, Albert's, usual chair beneath the caribou heads with ears missing.

Fielding's light fell on Virgil and me again, and this was nauseating because we could not manage to rise from the love seat; it was hopeless, everybody staring at Virgil climbing across my lap.

"Don't."

"Stop."

"Wait."

"Stop."

"Don't."

"Wait."

Luckily Tom came over to help. Tom seized Virgil's arm and hauled him off me. Shame at this gathered in Virgil, who mumbled, "What do you know, couldn't stand up, must be getting old or something, thanks, Tom."

"No problem."

"Yes, thank you," I said to Tom, who, perhaps for Virgil's benefit, said, "These antique chairs were built for smaller people, weren't they?"

"Sure were," I agreed.

"If you ask me, I think we ought to clear this place out and refurnish. Fix up these floors, knock out a few skylights," said Tom.

"Hmn," I said.

"I mean, the colors in here. What's so great about red? You know, studies have shown that colors have significant effects on mood. Did you know that?"

"I think I did."

"And red is, I'm not sure what exactly it is red supposedly does."

"Violence and aggression," I said.

"Is that right?"

"Of course in heraldic symbolism red is frequently associated with the monarchy."

"Interesting."

"As is purple. Here we see the three-way connection between secular power, the impassioned genitals, and the spilled blood of the Lord drunk by the faithful as Communion wine."

"I guess that's true," said Tom in the bright light from Fielding's camera. Fielding was becoming impatient; he peeked from behind the viewfinder and mouthed the words *Come on*. Max on his back heaved in oxygen. A short distance away Barry sat on the floor and clutched his head. Virgil beside me shivered and said, "Doug, I don't feel so good. Will you check my temperature?"

"Okay," touching my palm to his wet forehead. He was hot. "You're fine," I told him. But in the light he looked horribly unwell with his blue-white skin the color of a shaved puppy. Moisture emitting from him beaded up on his head where his hair was thinning at the crown. Openmouthed he looked about.

I understood then that he was growing sicker and might not live much longer.

The light beckoned. Fielding's hand kept waving. I got a supporting hold on Virgil's arm and off we went toward the wide center of the room, toward our Max. Brothers stood in a file on Virgil's left, and in another line on my right; behind were more with necks craned. Several along our way acknowledged us. Vaughan nodded and Eric motioned with his hand, a barely perceptible greeting. Phil, standing in line beside Gregory, whispered, as we passed, "Hey, Doug. Hey, Virgil."

"Hello, Phil," I said.

"Philip," whispered Virgil.

"Gregory," I then said.

"Doug, Virgil, hello," replied Gregory, and Virgil also nodded. Frank said:

"Boys."

"Frank," we said, going by.

Angus leaned in close as we walked past. "Doug, I need my belt sander back."

"Right. I keep forgetting. Sorry."

"Whenever you get a chance," Angus said as Walter, next in line after Angus, remarked obnoxiously, "Hey, Doug, are you still trying to figure out where we all come from?"

"Genealogy is the indigenous history of the Self," I told that jerk in passing.

To Virgil, though I know he has no particular interest in ancient heraldic artworks, I confided in a whisper, "Remind me to show you an amazing picture I found of a fourteenth-century boar *couchant* with wattled neck and the hind legs of a goat. It's Walter exactly."

"At least *you* don't have to sit next to the guy at dinner," said Virgil, huffy.

Fielding, meanwhile, crept backward as he filmed, establishing an enlarged perspective—the cinematic space dramatically unfolding, and so forth—squeezing more Max in the frame. Back Fielding went, three feet, five feet, ten, fifteen, steadily across the frayed carpet and onto hardwood floor, as if riding a dolly. I suppose it is inevitable that some youthful humorist would be unable to forgo crouching on all fours in Fielding's unwitting path.

The prankster this time was Jeremy. I could see it coming because of course I was squinting directly at Fielding retreating across the room and could make out, behind him, the small figure tiptoeing the long way around the ratty wicker chaise and the drop-leaf table holding the cannon glass paperweight collection. Virgil saw, too. It happened fast. Jeremy knelt on the cold floor. Snickering arose from various corners but no one said a word.

Fielding was absorbed in cinematography and wouldn't have heard anyway.

He panned onto Max. He raised a hand to calibrate focus. Max's eyes were shut but his mouth was open and his hands by his sides were clenched. Fielding focused on him. He stepped back. Stepped back again. Suddenly Fielding was going down over Jeremy and the camera's blinding light was zooming upward and away to spray whiteness across ceiling, a wall, the floor.

Equipment crashed and the camera light died. The room seemed to fall momentarily dark. From the darkness came a sound of wrestling and the ominous shouts of the night's first of three fights.

"You fucker!"

"Take it easy, man!"

"I'm going to strangle you!"

"It was a joke!"

"Are you mindless? Do you have any idea what you have done? Do you?"

"Don't push me."

"I'll push you. I'll push you if I want to push you, you unimportant fuck."

"Don't get mad!" Jeremy cried in a voice that sounded strangled. Then there was a noise: cloth ripping. Something weighty fell and the Doberman commenced barking insanely as Fielding harangued:

"How often do you think a shot like that comes along? How often?"

"I don't know! I'm sorry. Let go!"

"Never! That's how often a shot like that comes along. Never!"

Other brothers converged in a circle ringing the fighters. No one was butting in, yet; experience has proved that it is best to let physical disputes resolve themselves on the spot, rather than interrupt and create additional frustration and the lasting grudges that accompany smoldering tensions— unless there is peril of injury.

Fielding held Jeremy in a classic under-the-arm headlock. Close by the two men's feet lay that camera, irritant to all of us and a heap of parts now. Fielding, seeing it busted, went red in the brain. "You shit!" he yelled while dancing up and down with Jeremy's smothered head bobbing.

This was inauspicious. Fielding is hardly large, but he is

utterly self-centered and therefore disliked, therefore intimidating, and no one wished to challenge him. Who can predict what a narcissist will do in anger?

*"Aaaaghhh,"* Jeremy managed to say; and Fielding, squeezing him, made this speech: "What do you think? What do you *think*? I filmed you riding your bicycle and I filmed your sixteenth birthday and you can be damned sure I filmed it when you got back from the hospital and you were in remission and we were all here to celebrate your health and that was no joke, was it? Was it? Maybe you don't want anyone to care about that. Is that what you prefer? No troubling evidence that you are *alive* and have *feelings* and people who *love* you in spite of the fact that you are an immature *child* who doesn't know how to comprehend love? A little kindness would go a long way around here, but I suppose I can't expect you to have much regard for congeniality because obviously you're *lost* in an arrested world of lame jokes and *sick* tortures. And that goes for everybody!"—peering around the room at the amazed faces, raising his voice to cry above Gunner the attack dog's savage, intermittent barking—"In my mind there's a difference between friendly clowning and this kind of malicious assault on a person!" Bark. Bark. Bark. "Mature men ought to know this difference!" Bark. Bark. Bark. "Show some courtesy!"

He let go of Jeremy's neck. Jeremy, delivered from minor humiliation, collapsed before Fielding's feet. Fielding was becoming emotional, and, strangely, so were we.

He said to us, "I make documentaries because I love my

brothers. Is that wrong? Someone, tell me if it is wrong, because I feel ridiculous for even saying it."

He bent down, collected the smashed camera pieces. Nobody seemed capable, right away, of speech or action; it was a time for reflection on the complexities of our interdependence and the sorry indignities that pass as currency between us in lieu of gentler tender.

Fielding cradled his camera. Everywhere beneath the obscure light from twenty broken chandeliers, heads were bowed. Virgil laid his full weight on my arm; he leaned on me; and Maxwell, for the moment, was forgotten, though his breaths could be heard, along with Chuck's dog's periodic outbursts and Jeremy's sobs. Not yet seven o'clock and already someone had made someone else cry. The sad function of this—and there is, I believe, implicit in such dynamic enactments of taunting and submissive roles, a manifest, though hidden, *function*—the function of this is to ally disparate siblings within coherent factions characterized by age or friendship patterns (or some or other preexisting ideological or emotional attitude), and in this way to relieve the stresses that accompany explicitly *personal* self-presentations in a company as amorphously large as ours. The unconscious drive to assert autonomy through withdrawal into a prejudicial collective is counterintuitive but unexceptional; it can be seen at work during any polite cocktail party, whenever political or philosophical debates erupt, and guests begin either claiming or refuting intimacy with one another by announcing, "Yes! Yes! I agree with so and so."

Of course this is routine social behavior and everyone is familiar with it. Nor does the comparison with cocktail parties hold absolutely, since, as yet, that night in the red library, no cocktails had been poured.

Battle lines were forming anyway. Fielding in his rage had done Jeremy the valuable service of converting him from playful culprit to injured victim, two qualities practically everybody can empathize with.

Fielding had, in the process, gone too far in two directions. His anger was alarming, his reflexive petition for charity, sentimental. Here was the pathos of a man struggling to identify himself through artistic creation understood as a service, a gift to others—admittedly a beautiful and romantic formulation, though also abstruse and quixotic and, however sincerely expressed (our brother's earnestness in this matter was not, I think, at issue), difficult to sympathize with in any really tangible way; and Fielding's violence had without a doubt already made him a distinctly uncompelling object for sympathy or pity; and who among us wants love thrown in his face anyway? Jeremy's crying was growing louder and louder (he did seem badly hurt, Jeremy, rolling around on bare floor, as a man will when in spectacular pain), so that, in the end, after what seemed a long while, but was, actually, probably less than half a minute's worth of our standing there self-consciously wondering whom to blame for what and how to feel okay about it—in the end, our brother Fielding, who on any other night might have found twenty or thirty eager to champion his supposedly heartfelt artistic martyrdom—brother Fielding was, this night, pretty much without a prayer.

"Your movies are bad!" a voice called at him from the far side of the room.

"You use people and things and you don't care who gets hurt! Is that your idea of love?" heckled an unidentifiable other from the darkness over by Sociology.

"My camera! Oh, my poor camera. Look at my camera," the filmmaker grieved.

From the vicinity of the fireplace came a voice harsh and familiar to us all:

"Knock it off."

Who else but Hiram. Here he came on his walker, haltingly one-handing it along, lame and clattering and now giving, I thought, uncharacteristically generous counsel: "Look here, Fielding, it's not the end of the world. What is broken can be mended. A lot of people don't have movie cameras and they don't complain, they're happy. Perhaps you might take this opportunity to exercise some self-control. Stand tall and be a leader. Set an example the rest of us can follow." And then, gesturing toward Jeremy: "Someone help this unfortunate young person off the floor. Can't you see his suffering? Can't you hear his crying? How many nights have I spent listening to the dry whimpering of the young in this house? How many mornings have I woken to thoughts of death, the pounding of boots in the hall. I would offer our brother assistance myself, but, as you can see, this is not possible"—pausing to lean on his walker and wheeze a few breaths before raising his injured wrist for all to witness—"tonight I was almost murdered, and my hand has been destroyed."

Hiram's fist in the air was vermilion and swollen. Talking had fatigued him. With his good hand he gripped the walker, and his body collapsed heavily against its metal railing. Now with brittle hips he gave a push, and the walker scooted a tiny distance forward. Clack clack. Hiram held on. We watched him shuffle feet. Next he hoisted himself up. "Clear out of my way. I'm not in my grave yet, though I am sure there are many in this room who might wish I was," Hiram croaked. The Doberman—leashed in place to the art nouveau chair he'd overturned at the outset of Maxwell's screaming episode—barked a high-pitched bark, as if trumpeting Hiram's arduous journey around the reading lamps and across the room.

In the meantime, a small mob containing mostly twins convened around Jeremy. Matching hands reached out to palpate Jeremy's shoulders and his back and, very gently, Jeremy's head. Matching voices inquired, "Where does it hurt?" "Is it your neck?" "Are you able to breathe?" "Do you feel dizzy?" "What's your birthday?" "Jeremy? Look at me. Can you look at me? Jeremy, how many fingers am I holding up?"

"Kind of dizzy. January eleventh. Two," Jeremy said between sobs. Helping hands helped Jeremy stand, and he was able to walk enough to make it, with an escort, to the cigarette-burned purple divan, where he reclined, a velvet pillow supporting his head, his feet dangling off the end.

"Oohhh," he said.

This was no time to be playing doctor, but with Jeremy so helpless—he'd remembered his birthday incorrectly (it's the eighth or the ninth, I think) *and* miscounted Winston's fingers held only inches before his eyes (looked to be three from where I was standing, not two) and should *not* have been *walking*—and with Barry temporarily out of commission (precipitous double vision sending him to his back whenever he tried to get up), that is exactly what I decided to do. I honestly cannot say what possessed me, exactly. Jeremy's pain was, undeniably, great. It was true that the whole night lay before us, drinks and dinner. Shouldn't we all, under such circumstances, be happy? I saw Barry's black bag beneath a table—it must have been kicked there in all the commotion—and I thought it would be easy to locate the suitable anti-inflammatories or painkillers and administer to the lame and the halt. Medical ignorance did not seem an impediment. I was thinking, I think, that if I could get that doctor's bag and root around in it a minute, my hand would be guided.

While I was at it, I could maybe slip Virgil a tranquilizer. I know I had promised, earlier in the evening, that no such plan would cross my mind. But what can you do with a person as unrelaxed as Virgil? Why not give him a little candy to help him through the night?

How to persuade Virgil to go along with this. Virgil's aversion to health-care paraphernalia is well known. Getting the doctor's bag would not be simple. It was possible that I could release my grip on Virgil's arm, then violently wrench Virgil's hands free from my own, cast him off and abandon him, so to speak. How often had I promised myself, on these evenings of ours, a sabbatical from Virgil's clinging? But things are never so simple. We seem, Virgil and I, always to find one another. It is true that he craves sympathy. I imagine his anxiousness, his frailty, his bleak and misanthropic outlook, as intimations of a sophisticated personal style— Virgil's Artful Guardedness—evidence not of weakness but of thwarted vitality: Virgil's will to thrive masked by a public demeanor of hopelessness, inadequacy, emotional and moral dereliction. And I imagine, probably wrongly, that if I just push him, if I goad him in the right way and with the appropriate insistence, he will forswear this deception and fight his way through the range of his adult feelings, whatever they may be, rage, disgust, elation, gratitude; and, in gratitude, become the kind of person I need and want him to be, the kind of man I most desire for fellowship in this room peopled with loud, assertive types—a genuine and strong ally.

Tonight he was looking more and more sickly. His proximity was becoming stifling. I longed to break loose from him. If I did, if I left Virgil unattended, he would very likely fall dizzily to the floor, and if he did not fall down, he would certainly run away and lock himself in the rare-book room, and I would have to come after him and talk sweetly to him through the door, and then I'd want to beat the crap out of him.

"I want your help," I told him.

"What for?"

"To do something."

"What?"

"Will you help me?"

"It depends."

"Oh, come on, Virgil. I'm begging you. Christ. Jesus. I'm standing here holding on to you all night, keeping the bad spirits away, taking your temperature, being a friend. Do me a favor already."

"All right."

"We've got to get that doctor's bag. It's right over there. See it?"

"Wait a minute, Doug."

"Let's get the bag," tugging him toward the mahogany coffee table with leather satchel underneath, Virgil in tow but frantic.

"What are you going to do, Doug? Doug, what are you going to do?"

"Nothing."

"Don't you want to check on Max?"

"He's sleeping."

"Max isn't sleeping. His eyes are open. Look. He needs you."

"We'll check on Max in a minute. Now come on," yanking Virgil by the arm—hard.

"You want to give me an injection. Don't stick me, Doug. Please don't stick me," he whimpered. We were all tangled up with each other. My feet stumbled over his. He said, "Doug, I'm thirsty. I'm so thirsty."

I felt it important to hurry. Things seemed critical. Virgil's face wore a bad color. "Just a little farther, Virgil. Cooperate with me. Fortitude. I know you have it in you. Don't disappoint me, Virgil, and I'll bring you a drink."

"Oh, my God, I wish you wouldn't say that because you can't mean it. You know what I want."

It was true. I knew what he wanted and I wanted the same or stronger, and why wasn't the wet bar set up yet? Where were Clayton and Rob?

The doctor's bag lay almost within reach. Suddenly Albert over in his gigantic horsehair chair tapped a neighboring sofa leg with his blind person's long white cane—official notice that he was about to speak, three loud strikes, as always. Albert cleared his throat and addressed the entire room: "Are drinks being served? If it's no trouble, I'll have a gin and tonic. Gilbey's will do, and no twist, please. That is, if anyone is making a trip to the bar." Hiram, at that very moment "walkering" himself past Albert's chair, startled Albert by snorting, "Your stick's in the way. Move it or lose it."

"Unbelievable," Virgil sighed.

"He is a piece of work," I agreed.

"I love him, though," said Virgil.

"Yeah."

We resumed struggling toward the mahogany table defaced by coffee stains and water rings showing where people had spilled or placed glasses down time after time without a coaster. Virgil, still trying to pilot me away from the doctor's bag, wrapped his arms around my middle, pushed his face against my chest, and hugged tight; his feet dragged. At some point I could brook this no longer. Other people's terror is so exasperating. I carried him a final uneasy step or two before trying to wrestle free. I grabbed Virgil's shoulders and pushed him away and his arms flailed but he seized my coat sleeves then lost his balance and we almost toppled, but I caught him. Virgil was showing no respect for physical force in relation to weight distribution: he did not seem to care if he tripped us both and brought me crashing down on his head. How can a person be so heedless of his body? I warned Virgil, "Wait a minute. Stop. Think about what you're doing. Let me show you something. If you grab from the side and rotate your hips like that, we're both going to go down, and I'll probably get hurt but you'll definitely crack your skull on that lamp. See what I mean? Spread your feet. Wider. You want to give yourself a strong foundation."

"Like this?"

"Not exactly."

"How's this?" he whispered.

"No. You're making it more complicated than it needs to be. The basic principles are simple. Imagine yourself *rooted* to the floor."

"This way?"

"Lower."

"Okay?"

"Better."

"Now what?"

"Try pulling."

"Nothing's happening."

"Well, I'm resisting. But, you see, with your center of gravity dropped, your position remains secure, and you can exert great force without losing equilibrium. Go ahead, pull as hard as you can."

"I don't feel very good, Doug."

"Pull, Virgil. Remember, use your legs, not your back. Control the motion."

"Feel really woozy, Doug."

He'd sunk, now, to his knees, almost. Looking down, I saw Virgil's feet splayed far apart and his soft arms embracing me, holding on awkwardly. I could feel, through his clothes and through mine, Virgil's body's distressing warmth, its fever. I can't say it felt that bad.

"No more wrestling lessons, Doug. I don't like wrestling." He sounded out of breath. His voice was scarcely audible. A smell was rising from him.

"All right. But in the future if you're not going to wrestle correctly, don't wrestle at all, because you don't know what you're doing and you don't *think* about what you're doing, and this is precisely what happens every time we wrestle, you don't think, and that's how people wind up in the hospital. Let go of my leg."

"You're going to put the dope in me."

"I only want to look in the fucking doctor's bag. Virgil! Please!"

The magic word. He let go. He tipped sideways and

slumped to the floor with hands pressed between legs and his knees drawn close in a fetal ball, twitching.

I took a quick glance around the room. It would not do to be caught pilfering from the black bag. People wouldn't understand, and I could be criticized for invasion of privacy or some equally vague infraction.

I stepped over Virgil. Brothers ranged all around. The library was busy with activity. Barry on the floor rubbed his eyes and shook his head. Jeremy on the purple divan complained loudly, "My neck, my neck." Twins in pairs leaned over to stroke Jeremy's face and his hands. "You're going to be all right," soft voices assured him. Immediately to the left of this, Siegfried, Raymond, Milton, and others watched Fielding gesture pathetically with his camera parts—the viewfinder, the battery pack, the cracked film canister—holding up these pieces for inspection, showing the damage, telling and miming his role in the conflict, building a narrative. "I didn't mean to hurt him. I'm sorry if I hurt him. You've got to believe me. Do you believe me?" I looked away then, over to my right, and saw that Seth and Vidal and Gustavus and Clay had quietly turned away from Fielding, away from Jeremy, Max, Barry, and the rest, and had returned to, were preoccupied with, erotic pamphlets and broadsheets. "Have you ever used this position, Vidal?" Clay asked his older brother. Vidal peered over Clay's shoulder at Clay's crumbling, dated bestiality scene. "Which position? The 'Virgin in the Manger'?"

Quickly I snuck the doctor's bag from beneath the table. What was here? Syringes? Nothing but syringes? A little cotton, alcohol, bandages, a stethoscope, and a sampling of stoppered vials containing liquids.

Virgil twitched. I dug a hand in the bag and lifted out a fistful of loose, unwrapped, probably used needles, and also a selection of vials. I did not, in my hurry, have time to read their labels.

All these things I distributed into my inside jacket pockets.

I closed the black bag and slid it back in place under the coffee table. Then, on a lark, I brought the bag out and unzipped it, quietly, again. Stethoscopes are great amusement, I think. Who can resist a stethoscope? I hauled this one out and inserted its rubberized earpieces. That's when I noticed that I was, in fact, watched.

"Hello, Max."

The opiated stare of the botanist was on me heavily. We gazed at each other's face. I have to admit I was ready to turn away in sadness, or feelings very like sadness, when I saw Max's mouth fall open. Max's gray tongue came out and began licking. My tie had become wound about Max's neck. A problem? Max's arms and his hands were bony things reaching out from blazer and shirtsleeves pushed up and bunched in linen folds around the elbows. Max's legs showed below trouser cuffs hiked almost to the knees, well above the socks. Their thinness was alarming and unnerving, because unexpected. When had Maxwell grown so frail, so brittle and waxy? Was it the drug? He looked as if he had been tossed onto his back from a great height and broken. One black loafer—a black, tasseled loafer that appeared, from where I stood, brand-new, very nice and comfortable, obviously soft to the touch—was hanging almost off its foot. The handsome shoe dangled from my brother's toe.

"You look like you could do with a pick-me-up," I said to him. His mouth leaked a dry gurgle and I took this delicate noise as affirmation. Certainly Clayton and Rob would soon be setting up the bar. The problem with getting a drink around here is fighting through the crowd at the drinks table. Perhaps our blood familiarity permits styles of behavior that most of us would probably suppress in other, less intimate settings—that is, shoving, elbowing, light punching, and related aggressive gestures. It is rare, at our drinks table, that one hears the invitation "After you." For this reason I often buddy up to Spooner, who packs his own cognac. Live and let live. Spooner was nowhere in sight and Max's tongue was sliding farther and farther out of his mouth and Virgil was showing signs of a possible seizure in the works and Hiram was as usual chastising someone who did not deserve it, and Albert was whacking his cane on the furniture and Jeremy was sobbing. The time now was shortly after seven o'clock. The Doberman was howling and each new yelp reverberated wildly and unremittingly inside the manifold ceiling vaults above our heads, a chorus of barking. Suddenly Barry clutched his forehead and moaned loudly before collapsing backward in one more failed bid to rise up and see straight.

I said to Max, "Why don't I fetch you a nice piña colada? A frosty piña colada will take the edge off. What do you say? I'll get a straw so you can sip lying down. How does that sound? Piña colada?"

In fact, I was not confident that blender drinks—or straws, for that matter—would be available at our wet bar, but it was, I believed, important to make this empathic gesture toward Maxwell's interest in, and concern for, the tropics. A small deceit but a valuable one if it could in any way make Maxwell feel happier.

A short note on the subject of time. I have just said that the time was shortly after seven o'clock. I should more accurately say that I *judged* the time to have been shortly after seven o'clock. Time in the red library is forever a subjective construct. A proliferation of wristwatches would seem to argue possibilities for agreement on what time it is. However, the opposite is more truly the case. Analysis of the dynamics of male sibling interrelatedness will reveal puerile disputes over abstractions like "the time." A hundred or so watches new and old will report a spread of at least thirty or forty minutes before or past the hour. Such variability will, among men, occasion pride and combativeness over who's right and who's wrong. It is safer, as a rule, not to ask the time. Factor in the conspicuously divergent times given by the half dozen semifunctioning grandfather clocks stashed in assorted nooks and corners around here, and the question of *time* becomes extremely thorny. On these grounds and on others more personal (having to do with my own passion for avowedly romantic, nonmechanistic lifestyles in bygone eras, the days of kings), I prefer to *surmise* the hour by traditional means of cosmic observation. Our tall eastern windows offer beautiful access to the stars, planets, and moon in nightly migration across the sky. On chilly evenings when clear polar air blows the haze right out of this forlorn valley, then vistas seem measureless, the heavens boundless; the universe regains its majesty and I feel primed to drink John Barleycorn, put on the Corn King costume, and take on all comers in a battle to the death.

"Let's have a listen to that heart of yours!" I exclaimed to Maxwell. His eyes lolled in his head as I advanced toward him with the stethoscope. I meant no harm and am sure Max would've understood this had he been in his right mind. His head jerked back and his mouth opened wide to bare teeth. Trying to talk? I knelt beside him, leaned in close, and quietly, so no one would hear—Virgil was lying only a few feet away, at the edge of the carpet—whispered, "Maxwell, it's your brother Doug. You called my name. Don't be frightened. No one is going to hurt you. We grew up together. Remember growing up? Remember our room we shared with Virgil? Remember how we used to beat the daylights out of Virgil? Everything is going to be all right, Maxwell. What did you want to say to me?"

I took his sweating hand and held it, squeezed it, lightly, in order to calm him and reassure him, and he growled at me.

If you've ever been growled at by another person, you'll know how unsettling this can be.

"Please don't be unfriendly, Maxwell," I told him.

The stethoscope depended from my ears. My brother's dilated eyes watched it hovering in air above him. I shook my head—a small, rhythmic motion causing the instrument to swing back and forth in dreary light from lamps nearby. Barry's stethoscope glittered. Max, watching it zip along above his nose, smiled.

"You like that?"

Max looked happy. I dipped my head, raised and dipped. The stethoscope swept left then right, one way and the next, higher and higher before accelerating downward then streaking up again on elastic black tubing. Whoosh! Max's gaze did not leave it. I crouched on all fours, bobbed over him, peered into his laughing mouth filled with scum and spit. I could feel, faintly, on my own face, Max's exhalations. He gave off bitter odors. Dampness seeped from crotch to thighs across his trousers. "Oh, Jesus, you've gone and wet yourself," I sighed as, suddenly, Barry's weighty brass and steel stethoscope hurtled down along its crescent path and struck Max cleanly on the nose—*thunk*. Immediately I pressed a hand over his mouth. For Max to cry out and be heard at large would be inconvenient as hell considering the pilferage stashed in my jacket pockets and the fact that I would doubtless be rebuked for harmful negligence regarding Max's pitiable state, his every breath being precious, etc., etc. The general level of contentiousness around here is its own advertisement for discretion. Already footsteps approached from the direction of the card catalog. I spoke quickly and quietly into Maxwell's ear. "I see no reason for a scene. I'm sorry about your nose, but I can tell you right now that if you decide to make trouble, it will not be happy for you."

Then the footsteps were here and a voice was saying, "Hey, guys. What's going on? Doug, is everything all right? Is Max all right?"

"Hello, Bertram. Yes, Max is fine. He's feeling much better. How are you?"

"I'm okay. Doug, why do you have your hand over Max's mouth? Is that a good idea?"

"His tongue was acting strange, Bertram. I thought I'd try to calm it down."

"Like that?"

"Touch can be very healing."

"I know, but it doesn't look like he's getting any air. I think you ought to remove your hand, Doug."

"In a minute, Bertram, in a minute. Max is fine. He's breathing through his nose and his tongue is calming down considerably."

"No, Doug. Look. His nose is bleeding."

It was true. A hideous red stream oozed from Max's nostril to gutter up against my hand and wash down the sides of Maxwell's dirty, unshaved face.

"Here, use these," said Bertram, offering tissues in a

pocket-size wrapper. I wiped Max, and Bertram said, "Tilt
his head so the blood can clot."

"Like this?"

"Don't let the head hang back. You can compress the ar-
tery and cause a stroke. Careful! You're going to strain his
neck!"

"Relax, Bertram."

"Let me do it, Doug. I get nosebleeds myself. I know exactly what to do."

"You get nosebleeds?"

"I get them in winter when there's dry heat. Move your
hand." He knelt and reached behind Maxwell's neck, cradled
Max's head in his hands.

"Got him?" I asked.

"Yes."

"Do you have any more tissues? These are about used
up." I held wadded, bloody paper. No trash can was in sight.
More blood flowed. I tossed the tissues under a chair. Red
filled Maxwell's ears and a small red tide matted his hair
and dribbled from there onto carpet. His shirt collar was
stained, and my tie, as far as I could tell, was wet around the
neck and probably ruined. Was there any point in untying it
and slipping it off Max? Perhaps. It could be dry-cleaned. I
know a dependable cleaner who often has success with difficult stains. I suggested to Bertram that it might be prudent
to remove the tie from Maxwell; then I reached in and got to
work. This tie is fashioned from a superior, floral-print silk
that achieves an especially fine, compact knot. If you hitch it

tight, it'll stay tight and it'll look good, no matter what. The knot around Max was remarkably firm. I tried getting a purchase on a fold of loose silk, but had no luck and so tried easing the intact knot down the tie's slender length—to slide it down Maxwell's shirtfront and in this way open and enlarge the "noose." This did not work either. The knot would not yield. I was smearing my brother's blood on my hands, and the stethoscope was rocking and pitching over Maxwell's face, and I felt oppressed by the stupidity and smallness of life. Bertram said, "What's bugging you tonight, Doug?"

"This is my tie. It's my favorite tie. He took it without asking and now it's ruined."

Bertram leaned close to inspect the bloody tie and said, "It's got a lot of maroon in it already, and it's pretty dark overall. Plus, it's not glossy. The weave will conceal discoloration. These earth tones might even be enhanced. One thing you can do is, when you're putting it on, you can fiddle with the knot, to hide the stains. I had a tie with water spots on it once, and I found that if I tied it just so, all the water spots would be out of sight."

Need I say it hurt me to think of my weary, middle-aged brother standing before a fogged-up bathroom mirror, carefully, deliberately, obsessively tugging at soiled neckwear? I had a vision of him with uncombed hair and a misbuttoned shirt, his crummy tie flapping, and with bloody tissues stuffed up his nose, as he readied himself for a horrible new day.

In fact Bertram has been, on every occasion I can recall,

clean, presentable, freshly shaved, and dressed in clothes that look ironed. But you never know. The lining could be out on his coat, and his pockets frayed, so that money spills through the holes. His loafers might be on third or fourth soles beneath trouser cuffs held in place with staples. On these first cold evenings in autumn, it is easy for me to imagine such decadence. Outside there is always the wind. Our rows of gaunt, denuded trees present their broken limbs as, now and then, scattered fallen leaves bluster upward in brown or reddish, swirling twisters that catch, then fling shut, loudly and abruptly, again and again, the unpainted wooden gate that opens onto the rose garden. It was, I believe, someone's job one summer to go out and repair the latch on that gate. Nothing was ever done, and now ages have passed and no one seems to notice or much care about the rose garden gate as it slams and slams in the dark. At this point it's just one worry among many. In strong winds the library's windows rattle thunderously, and it seems certain they will burst and rain glass on our heads. Drafts pour in. Even with Hiram's great fire roaring in the hearth—and with one of Clayton's tasty whiskey cordials in hand—it is possible, in nighttime, to feel a chill, the brisk fluttering against one's skin of subtle, icy gusts. What must it be like, in this bitter season, to inhabit the shabby tent city that covers the meadow beyond the wall? From time to time I will happen to peek out a rattling window and glimpse the trash-can fires here and there illuminating bleak lean-tos and crouched, windblown figures. Invariably I contemplate the happy fortune we in this room share; and I will offer, almost always, a silent prayer of thanks; and once in a while, in my prayers, I might name one or several of my brothers, those suffering inordinately.

I stared down at blood spilled on my hands and my tie, at the blood still trickling from Maxwell's busted nose, and said to Bertram, "Why don't I go see if Clayton and Rob can spare a few cocktail napkins."

"Good idea."

"Can I bring you anything from the bar?"

"Seltzer."

"Not drinking tonight, Bertram?"

"Better not, I think. You know how it is."

"Absolutely. One seltzer, coming up," I said, extracting the stethoscope's rubber plugs from my ears. My ears were sore from wearing them. Bertram said, "Bring me some peanuts if there are any," and I told him I would. I coiled the stethoscope and shoved it into an outside coat pocket, then headed off in the direction of Early Modern Architecture and Decorative Arts. That's where our bar is located.

Along the way I had to step over Virgil. He lay coiled in a ball at the edge of the carpet. His eyes were shut—tight. He must have fallen into nightmares, judging from the way his body twitched all over. I stole a pillow from a nearby chair and, gently, so as not to disturb his rest, slid it underneath Virgil's head.

"Sweet dreams, little brother. Don't let the bedbugs bite.

But if they do, squeeze them tight, and we'll have them for supper tomorrow night," I recited softly to him while his hands and his feet shook.

If he did not wake in a while—if Virgil did not wake up feeling rested—we could always try, later in the evening, a moderate dosage of one or another of Barry's intravenous medications. The night was young. I took one final look back toward Bertram, kneeling, holding Max's head in his lap. Maxwell gazed up at his brother's face, as Bertram, with one hand, rubbed the top of Maxwell's head.

I turned away and stepped across Virgil and off the worn-down Bokhara, onto floorboards running the length of this room clogged with siblings prowling for seats. What a muddle. The day's last sunlight was gone, long departed; the eastern windows were dark, and in the library's darkness it was hard to say for sure who was who until you came close or made out the voice. This was not easy because now someone had unlocked the stereo cabinet and music was loudly erupting from speakers hooked up in the bookshelves. I'm fond of lieder but only now and then and never during the cocktail hour. The splendor of the human voice lifted in song is undeniable; nevertheless, we have in our red library enough raised voices. The familiar clamor of many spirited conversations is, in its own way, I think, a kind of music. Not that I particularly wanted to talk to anyone. I just wanted my drink. It's always a challenge to cross this room without falling prey to some lout with an opinion about life. The best strategy is to assume an attitude of urgency, walk fast, and refuse eye contact or any intimation of recognition when your name is called. On the other hand, it's never good to seem unfriendly. As I was saying, I wanted my drink.

That said, allow me to skip over the night's trivial encounters, the "Hey, how are you?" conversations and other conversations nearly avoided, all the little tête-à-têtes and informalities that ensue whenever you take a stroll through our balding fraternity of blue blazers and wool cardigans, haggard faces and potbellies and yellowing teeth. What can be said about a trip to the bar?

Gusts shook the windowpanes. Gunner barked. The rose-garden gate slammed, reopened, slammed again. Our twenty golden chandeliers' innumerable tiny bulbs blinked off then on, off then on. Their wiring is ancient and questionable, and the fuse box is overloaded and a fire hazard besides. This room always feels haunted after dark. You never know when a wall-mounted tiger will catch your eye. Suddenly, in one startling heartbeat, in a trick of failing lamplight, the tiger will seem alive. Surprise! Then you notice its pallid, gray furlessness and its blackened hole for a mouth, and the opacity of the glass "cat's-eye" eyes. You might think then of your own hair loss, failing vision, periodontal problems. Where was that drink?

Across the room. Unfortunately, before I could set sail for the drinks table, I had to contend with Roger coming toward me in his cowboy boots. Roger swears incessantly

and excitedly about things that bother him; he's a com-
plainer. To avoid him I had to tack left—away from the bar
and toward the *Life* magazines. This took me past Jeremy in
his agony on the purple divan. Of course I had those syringes
in my coat pocket. It was not the moment for recreation with
needles, veins, strange medicines. Twins in their protective
swarm huddled over Jeremy, blocking him from view except
for one foot sticking out between someone's legs. "Put a couple
of these in his mouth," one twin exhorted another. Aspirin? I
know I said I would not recount the night's petty encounters
and conversations. Then again, who knows what fragment of
dialogue, offhand gesture, inadvertent slight, so forth—who
knows what exactly will, in retrospect, turn out to have been,
in some unforeseeable way, in the end, meaningful? I veered
away from the purple divan and forged a path among towering
open stacks. It was good to see a few readers leaning against
shelves. One was Larry, and he had in his hands our well-
thumbed study of salvation by foreordainment, Bartlett and
Gibson's *Infralapsarianism in Everyday Life*. As I passed him, he
looked up from the page.

"Doug, got a minute?"

"Sure."

"I'm having a little problem with God."

"What's up?"

"Life after death."

Two brothers nearby, Simon and Henry, also reading, apparently, Christian History and Theology, glanced up at

this, peered in our direction, listening in. Larry did not seem to mind or notice; he said, "Lately I have this feeling that life is very short, Doug."

He took a deep breath. His face was not clean and wore the drained, unsettled expression of a man needing sleep.

"How old are you, Larry?"

"Thirty."

"I see."

"Everything's rushing by, you know?"

"I do."

"I thought by now I'd have some idea how to not feel so afraid," he said, and grinned. Was this one of those occasions for prayer? A brief and silent prayer for the happiness and well-being of a troubled younger brother? I asked him, "How afraid are you?"

"Very afraid."

"Insomnia?"

"Yes."

"Loss of appetite?"

"Yes."

"Inability to concentrate?"

"Yes."

"Dry mouth?"

"Yes."

"Intermittent hyperventilation?"

"Definitely."

"Frequent urination? Persistent suicidal ideation?"

"Mmn."

Overhead lights flickered off, on, off. It is forever like night in the stacks. Larry's unclean face hovered close to mine. His voice sounded weak, sickly, and his breath smelled like milk.

"Do you ever have these feelings, Doug?"

"No."

Why did I tell him this lie? Now he would suppose his problems were unusual and grave, rather than ordinary and average, and he would feel alone with them. He looked stricken. It's best to try not to cause pain, but pain seems to happen despite the most friendly intentions. Suddenly I was glad I had Barry's syringes in my coat pocket—though I am not sure why I thought of the syringes at that moment.

"Oh," Larry said sadly. And closed Bartlett and Gibson's *Infralapsarianism in Everyday Life,* gently because like so many of our best-loved volumes, its binding was cracked and splitting. He replaced it on the shelf, between *The Puritan Ordeal* and *The Mirror and the Lamp.* Our misshelving problem was clearly reaching a crisis point.

I should say right now that I am not, as a rule, as a *general* rule—and by general I mean that for the most part the rule holds, though isn't it true that rules are, as they say, made to be broken?—I am not, as a rule, much of a drinker. So I am always mystified when I consider that, at least among certain of my relations in this room, I have a reputation as one. And for what? A few broken chairs and the odd pointed remark late at night?

In this way are we, in our most emotional, our most vulnerable moments, our moments of comradeship, of celebration and even passion, misunderstood.

My "reputation" aside, I felt that the bar would be a safe haven—our sole refuge from the incurable hopelessness lurking inside so many of us in this scarlet place, lurking, as it were, in the room itself. With this in mind I said what I needed to say to make Larry feel a tiny bit confident about the likely afterlife prospects for his soul. "Look here, friend. You don't need to worry too much about the Doctrine of Predestination, because you've got the Doctrine of Good Works to go with it. The chosen few are known by their actions on earth. If you're so damned nervous about the everlasting future, why not try being a better person?"

Next I manufactured some justification for leaving. Maybe I spoke truthfully and said I was getting a drink and it'd been nice talking but really I was in a hurry. My chest felt tight and I could not stop biting my lower lip and my mouth tasted like chalk. I could not see the bar—Archaeology and Anthropology of the Near Middle East obstructed the view to it. I heard men crying out their orders for whiskey sours, imported beers, vodka tonics, dry martinis. I could hear Clayton's ice pick stabbing ice, and then that thrilling, unmistakable clatter: Clayton's perfectly hewn ice chunks dropping into tumblers set up on the bar and ready to fill. Ping! My throat tightened when I heard that reverberant, beckoning sound, our Waterford highball carillon rousing us from chairs and sofas, rousing us and distracting us from, I suppose, the stressful discussions we had, that wintry night, gathered together to undertake.

I mean about the missing brass urn. The urn and the ashes deposited therein.

No one was altogether certain who'd last seen the urn. Jason, once, long ago, reported a sighting over near where maps of the world are stored in drawers, but it wasn't, it turned out, there. And sometime back Paul suggested looking in the gloomy alcove packed with patriotic music-hall songs in their archival boxes: a thorough search turned up nothing. A while later suspicion fell on Siegfried for possibly melting the urn and incorporating it in one of his biomorphic sculptures. This was unlikely. Siegfried does not work in brass; he prefers steel commandeered from the derelict mills in the valley—it's the political part of his artistic vision. Of course there were those charcoal drawings hanging in the tower, where Eli keeps his drawing studio. These illustrations are brittle with age, and slightly fanciful in that the "urn" depicted in them wears no handles and is embellished with pornographic reliefs. It has long been agreed, among most of us at least, that the genuine article features no lurid ornamentation, and it is therefore held that Eli's childhood still lifes in black and white say more about our solitary brother's oedipal struggles than about any "authentic" funerary object—a shame, since pictorial representation might've helped sort out all the confusion over what the urn looked like. Don't get me wrong. We had a pretty good idea. It stands a foot in height, approximately. Above the pedestal the urn has a width of two or three inches. The vase gracefully widens as it rises, growing in diameter before again narrowing, as urns do, beneath the lip. An opposing pair of angular "coffeepot" handles are the only elements on this modest vessel that show appreciable detail work; they're cast with a shallow, free-form motif resembling engraved paisley. The lid is unadorned and the base also is quite plain. Total weight with contents: ten pounds. Tarnish colors it.

"It's nice to have everyone together again, isn't it?" a voice near me said. I turned and saw, in the shadows, a man bearing flowers. This man said, "All the old faces. All the familiar voices."

"Hello?"

"It's me, Doug. It's William."

"William!"

"Don't be frightened. I brought these," he said, stepping partway out from darkness with pale flowers held before him. "Lilies brighten a room."

"Yes," I agreed.

"Take them."

"Me?"

"Put them out on a table, somewhere in the light where people can enjoy them."

"Are you sure?"

"Why not?"

"You brought them, William. Wouldn't you like to find a

spot for them? Let everyone know you brought flowers. I'm sure it will mean a lot."

"I'd rather not, Doug. I don't think I can bear to talk to everyone right now. Maybe later"—sighing.

"I understand."

"Take the flowers? Please?" he said, and offered me these lilies. I accepted and told him, "They're very beautiful. You're kind to bring them. Thank you, William."

"You're welcome, Doug." He retreated into the shadows. His retreating voice said, "You look good, Doug. Life is treating you well. Let's chat sometime."

Then he was gone behind European Folklore and Mythology, and I clutched the lilies he had brought for us.

In the library's open spaces men tramped singly or with buddies toward the drinks table. Others already with drinks stood drinking. They were lucky to have these drinks. By now the press around the bar would be enormous, five guys deep at least. It would take an eternity to get served. Clayton and Rob would've poured the last Johnnie Walker Black and there'd be nothing remaining but Johnnie Walker Red, if that, or maybe Four Roses brand, one of the gallon discounts that are admissible late at night but which you never want in the beginning. That's the way life goes around here. The blinking lights. The dry taste in the mouth. The body's craving need for something cold and warm at the same time.

Out into the milling crowd I hurled myself, out in search of a suitable vase for William's gift. The lilies with their long, thick stems, their lush, drooping blooms, required a large, heavy vessel—precisely what I could not locate.

"Does anyone know where I can find a vase that'll hold these?" I asked a group loitering around the Native American stone-tool collection in its metal and glass display case. Dennis shrugged and Noah said, "Sorry." Jim, who often does not speak, even when spoken to—he's a contemplative Buddhist—suggested, "Try over by the African masks."

Eventually one of us was going to crash down his glass or an ashtray too hard on that stone-tool display table and there would be a mess. I said, "You guys, be careful using that as a table because it isn't designed to support weight."

I did not mean to scold my brothers, but what can you do when people have no sense?

"Seen a vase, anyone?" I asked another bunch as I hurried past their leather sofa and chairs pulled up close in a circle.

"Not me," Lewis said.

"Maybe on the mantel," said Drake.

Then Lewis asked, "Have you checked the telephone table?"

"Which telephone table?" I asked him.

"The black one."

"I'll try there," I said. Then advised, "Take off your shoes if you're going to put your feet on the furniture because you'll scuff the leather."

On my way across the room I hurried past Barry on the floor. Violet hematomas colored the skin beneath Barry's eyes. Nobody was tending to the doctor. Presumably this was because he was a doctor and could look after himself.

I made a mental note to look in on him after I got rid of the flowers and picked up a toddy from the bar, that is, if he was still not moving.

"Excuse me," I said then as I elbowed past Richard, walking quickly toward me without looking where he was going. "Oh, I'm sorry, Doug. I didn't see you," Richard apologized, and I told him, "Open your eyes and pay attention before you hurt someone, okay?"

"Having a bad night, Doug?"

I considered. "No." Then considered further. "Maybe." After another moment's thought, I said, "The noise in here is getting on my nerves."

He nodded his head, as if in agreement, and I realized he wasn't agreeing; his head always bobs up and down because he has no control over the muscles in his neck; it's a neurological disorder, not unlike Tourette's, though much milder and without the obsessive, repetitive vocalizing. Symptoms include subtle motor perseveration affecting the upper torso and, when Richard is greatly agitated, the limbs; and, though benign, this is disconcerting to watch.

Affably, irritatingly, metronomically, Richard's head bobbed. "Don't like the music, Doug?"

"The music is pleasant but it's too loud. Why do those guys need to crank up the stereo like that? And Chuck's dog is driving me nuts. Can't he teach it to shut up? A person can't think with that barking."

"The dog is just excited and happy to be a dog. He'll calm down eventually."

"Let's hope so for his sake," I said, contemplating the needles and the vials hidden in my coat pocket. It would not be difficult to dispatch Gunner for the night, or, for that matter, longer.

Up, down went Richard's head. The sight of this filled me with loathing. "Richard, I'd love to stay and chat, but I've got to find a vase and water for these lilies." Already the flowers' lengthy stems appeared to be wilting. But they weren't wilting. They were bent, because I had gripped them tightly and crushed their stalks. I never was much good with plants. I tried cradling the crooked lilies, tenderly as if they were a child in my arms. I feared damaging the blooms. The blooms were heavy and sagged downward. What was the proper way to carry a spray of blooming lilies?

Upside down, as Parisians do! Held this way, with my arm at my side, the lilies cascaded almost to the floor. My walking style involves some rhythmic arm swinging; I had to exercise control in order not to kick the swaying petals with my shoes. I extended my right arm and held the flowers away, at an angle, thirty degrees or more from my side. My left hand I stowed in my sport coat's outside pocket, along with the stethoscope coiled there; pliant tubing gave this hand something to keep busy with as I shuffled across the room. I had the creeping feeling, as I scouted around for a roomy vase, of a kind of theatrically extreme body consciousness—as if my affected, wary attentiveness to movement and positioning, vis-à-vis flowers, somehow invited my brothers' stares. A bouquet invariably draws attention to its holder. Still, I felt edgy and ill at ease, when Seamus, who was eating a piece of cheese, called out, his mouth full, "Hey, Doug, you're dragging those on the rug."

"Fuck off, Seamus. Why don't you help me find a vase instead of stuffing your face. What are you drinking?"

"Vodka."

"Give me a sip."

"Sorry, man. Get your own."

"Come on, Seamus. A sip?"

"I had to stand in line for this, Doug."

Why argue? I could see that Seamus's tumbler was all but drained. He was down to broken ice. A full-strength libation, mixed to order by the excellent Clayton, was what the onset of night called for. And it was, in the deepest sense, night. Freezing drafts seeped in. Gales outside gained swiftness. Damn that garden gate. Seamus raised his vodka glass, and ice clinked down the glass toward his mouth as, cruelly, he drank.

"Go easy on that stuff," I advised him, and he replied drolly, "That's like the pot calling the kettle black, isn't it, Doug?"

Here was a perfect instance of an untoward personal criticism offered in a somewhat inappropriate setting. Family affairs are always tiresome. There's nothing new about that. Yet there was no reason for Seamus to manifest his discomfort by handing out unsolicited character assessments. What number drink was Seamus on? He could easily have tossed one back at the drinks table before carrying away this sweaty, empty vodka clutched in his hand. Or he might've thrown down several *immediately*. Though it is, I can assure you, a chore to get more than two glasses lined up on our folding-table bar. The jostling of the crowd. Voices hollering their multiple orders. I like to ask for my usual double, plus some not-too-sweet mixed drink, to nurse in private. What's so wicked about that?

Seamus's face as he swallowed his last taste of watery vodka had its familiar worried look, the thin gray lips pressed firmly together, eyes reddish and glancing nervously in the direction of our bar. He was getting anxious, I guessed, about the prospect of more to drink and how long it would take to get it. He was not paying attention to me in the least, when I asked him, "Do you think our garden wall is high enough to keep people from entering the grounds?"

"People?" he said in a voice that sounded blurry and unconcerned. He peered down into the vodka glass—intently, as if maybe looking to discover something interesting among the puddling ice bits. Perspiration made Seamus's wide, round face glisten. He looked as if he might have come from a sauna. He sighed, "Did you hear the news about Russel?"

"What news?"

"I don't have this from the horse's mouth, but apparently there's something wrong with Russel's throwing arm."

"Oh, no."

"The arm and shoulder are so vulnerable to injury at Russel's age."

"How old is Russel?"

"Couldn't tell you, exactly. We're not getting any younger, any of us."

"That's a fact."

"Do you ever feel old yourself, Doug?"

"How do you mean?"

"Old, old."

"I occasionally have trouble getting out of bed in the morning, if that's what you mean."

"Because I was wondering if we could count on your help if the team needs it next Sunday afternoon at three against the Episcopal Ministers."

"It's been years since I've played, Seamus. I wouldn't even know how anymore."

"You were a top player once, Doug. You were a star. Father always said you were best."

There followed, at this, an interval of silence between us, after which Seamus went on, "Anyway, no one cares anymore about that ridiculous blunder in that unimportant championship match. Fumbles are part of the game. It's a shame when a team captain drops the ball in his own end zone just as the clock is running out, but that's fate, what's over is over, what's done is done, there's no going back and what's the point in picking at a sore spot? Everyone agrees if you'd had better blocking, things would've turned out differently. You took some quality hits and there's nothing more challenging than holding on to a wet ball, and the playing field was damp that day if I recall. At any rate it was a long time back and we've all put it out of our minds." Seamus gazed sleepily off toward the drinks table. He rambled on, "Talent like yours never really goes away. It's like riding a bicycle. Promise me you'll consider it, Doug. With you calling the plays and throwing the long ball, we could have the upper hand against the Ministers."

I told Seamus that I wasn't sure it was a good idea for me to play ball, though I was flattered he'd asked and I'd think about it as long as it was understood I wasn't making any commitments. "I barely find time in my schedule for the genealogical survey I've been working on. You'll be interested to know, Seamus, that I've recently discovered a namesake of yours in a ship's registry. Not, I might add, the first such ship's registry I have encountered in my researches concerning our family. At any rate, there's a Seamus in the registry for a voyage out of Portsmouth bound for the Ivory Coast and from there with its cargo, so called, to the New World. In the year 1811. Perhaps you'd like to stop by my study area later, and I'll show you your name. It's right there in the log. It's clearly legible. How about that?"

Seamus said, "Doug, forget that family history crap and come out Sunday and tug on the old jersey. It'll make you feel like a boy again, believe me. And, Doug, don't worry about the rush. With Gregory at the line of scrimmage, no Episcopal Minister will lay a hand on you."

"Gregory is an Episcopal minister."

Again Seamus gazed down into his vodka glass and, seeing its emptiness, sighed. In a weary voice he told me, "Whatever else you might believe about Gregory, he's loyal to family. He blocks for us."

All this time while talking and listening to Seamus, I was also hoping to myself that this man would not succumb to one of his narcoleptic interludes. For this especially was the time, true night and the light in the red library dreary and thin. Seamus was, I felt, a bit heated up over certain issues, issues that could be considered highly charged, emotionally charged and capable of sending my brother into the narcoleptic's reflexive, precipitous sleep. It doesn't take much in the way of sorrow or distress to knock him out. There was, for instance, that troubling question of Russel's arm in relation to next Sunday's match. This was clearly a source of worry for our whole team. Seamus, in particular, seemed to feel a heavy burden of collective anxiety. Russel's injury was a reminder, to Seamus and the rest of us, of the sadness and frustration that accompany aging. Then there was Seamus's repressed rage and disappointment with me for letting the team down in the past, not to mention the extreme tension that must have been occasioned by what I took to be a narcissistic dilemma. I'm referring to Seamus's recollection of father's admiration for my throwing ability. This must've pained my brother—notice his attempt to recover self-esteem by proxy: that unconvincing affirmation of Gregory's team spirit. Probably Seamus's upbeat assessment of Gregory's personality could be attributed to "first drink" enthusiasm for the night ahead and all the fun we would have together in the red library. This, then, would explain the disillusionment and depression triggered by the sheer fact of Seamus's barren, empty cocktail glass, his searching recognition of its watery emptiness.

As I was saying, it doesn't take much to deliver my brother into a deep, imperturbable sleep.

Seamus's eyelids fluttered. Men abroad in the room's lamplit distance were indistinct wandering figures. Some idled in the shadows as dialogues went on concerning business transactions or the unsightliness of someone's clothes or what hour dinner might finally be served since it was getting late, approaching eight already and high time for another round. "What're you having?" could be heard, answered with:

"Gin."

"Sherry, please."

"A glass of white."

"Another bourbon and water on the rocks if it's no trouble, Clayton, you can make that a tall one."

The festivities were gearing up. With the usual exception of the twins, groups of talking brothers were nebulous and permeable; in other words, drinkers with their drinks came and went from small cluster to small cluster until there were no more separate clusters, only a dense, chattering, semicontinuous current of bodies around the room and past the bar. Gentlemanly footfalls rumbled. Someone had turned the music loud but our voices rose louder. Who can abide these unquiet hours before dinner is wheeled out and arranged in trays on the oak table beneath the rose window that faces down on dead topiary?

Under moonlight our old trees take scary shapes. It's better, I think, to stay away from windows and not look down on those twisted silhouettes of animals and birds that seem to scream at you from leafless perches. Of course it's only wind screaming as usual through branches that creak, snap off, drop to the ground. I have suggested taking the ax—or a chain saw?—to the entire, warped grove, but no one will hear of this. "We could burn off the stumps, roll the grass, string a net, and play lawn tennis," I once proposed to a crowd seated around a low table spread with foreign-language periodicals. To which someone, it was Forrest if I recollect, looked up from Italian *Vogue* and replied, "In this wind?"

I looked back toward Seamus and saw that he was swaying in place, as if he were himself a kind of tall, old, bare tree, windblown and bending forward precariously with head down. His eyes were shut or almost shut; their lids fluttered. Backward Seamus leaned. His feet—in supple brown shoes—remained anchored. That glass was in his hand. It might've been wise to reach out and take this empty glass before Seamus let it drop, but Seamus's arms were waving, and once this begins it is best to avoid disturbing him because reckless arm gestures mean he is fast asleep on his feet and may not respond nicely to touch. An episode like this can last a few minutes or several hours, during which time Seamus, for reasons no one understands, will attempt to pick his way across the room through open stacks to the bathroom.

"Seamus is asleep again," I whispered to Arthur passing by on the long march toward the bar. Arthur turned to James, next in line, and advised him, "Seamus is asleep. Watch out."

In this manner word went out and Seamus was given leeway to swing his arms wildly. The sight of this filled me with guilt for all the things I could not put right simply by loving my brothers as they tottered about or collapsed to the library floor. Max, for one, had not budged from his spot on the carpet. There he was on his back with arms flung out and with shoes half on and half off. The blood had dried and Max was resting comfortably, watched over by Bertram waiting patiently for me to bring him a seltzer.

Close by was Virgil. Virgil had drawn himself into a cozy ball around that embroidered pillow I'd given him earlier. I could not see whether he was trembling. He hugged his pillow and looked contented.

Not so our Barry. Barry's whole head was bruised. He made intermittent, quite loud gurgling noises. His glasses had settled unevenly across the ruby bridge of his nose. Coins had spilled from Barry's trouser pockets and were scattered brightly around on the carpet.

No one at large paid these three men any attention. That's because—it should be plain by now—someone or other is always falling sick or having a spiritual awakening, and it's nothing unusual to step over that person lying on the rug and clutching a pillow as if for sweet life. This is not to say that if we must occasionally step over each other, we do not also cherish each other. On the contrary. Large families are a lot like small communities. We exist in relation to others. One learns to respect or at least tolerate one's neighbor's way of life, and also to refrain, whenever possible, from imposing oneself and becoming a nuisance. Otherwise, things get too appalling. For instance: Seamus, his arms waving hysterically for balance, deep asleep with eyes closed tight. Off Seamus went, out across the Bokhara, blazing a crooked trail around wide-backed mahogany chairs, in and out of that packed queue, his mates on their way to get more drinks. How can Seamus know his way to the bathroom? I can't answer that question except to venture that it seems likely that the sleeper's unconscious mind holds introjected "maps" of well-known environments; perhaps, in this way, Seamus *dreams* his way to the bathroom. That night, Porter, Andrew, Foster, and a half dozen others all swiftly leapt clear of their brother's oncoming fists; and Porter, jumping backward, knocked over a card table. The table tipped; men's voices cried out; Porter stumbled; the table crashed, and Seamus vanished into Civilizations and Empires of the Late Middle Ages; more voices; a new round of barking. Appalling, as I was saying. Noises came from everywhere, and the chandelier bulbs overhead flashed off, on, off, on, like playhouse lobby lights signaling act one. What a sad theater ours would be, with its inaccessible bar and its fire-hazard electrical circuitry and the cracked ceiling vaults and ripped curtains and the cigarette-burned seats, and the people and things constantly tumbling over and breaking

on the floor. It's enough to make you hate mankind. I sometimes imagine our red library as a kind of bleak and unruly
interpersonal anxiety zone. Emotions heat up and tempers
break out in real disputes that have their roots in a hundred
contingent histories of the standard childhood competi-
tions, degradations, reparations, punishments, tortures—
all the gory excitements of pain and power that seem, in
retrospect, so ineluctably linked with childish fantasies
about manhood. Screaming and crying were the routine
bedlam of our bedtimes, drowning out the crickets and the
pounding wind outside, but never the voices of older brothers who taunted, "Had enough, you little worms? Father
can't help you now!" It was Zachary who perfected the art
of the red belly, that scrubbing technique, the wire hairbrush on Virgil's bare white skin. Poor Virgil, pinned down
by Zachary's hands to our shared bunk bed's bottom mat-
tress. I held my eyes closed and pretended to sleep and did
nothing, night after night. It grieves me to think back now
over old boyish stuff, all the bad times made more bitter in
memory by the absence in this strangling red library of
a serene corner to hide out in, of a comfy chair that gets
enough light for reading without strain, of a taste of unstale
air to breathe. It's shocking, isn't it, how the dreadful circumstances of one's life grow to feel, simply because one
knows them, perfectly normal. Lost games, stolen toys,
handed-down clothes that never fit. I love my brothers and
I hate their guts. Me! Me! our voices all seem to shout—as if
we were not a true community united in blood and spirit,

instead a common mob intent on nothing more than the next drink, the next mouthful of food. I love my brothers and I hate my brothers. Most of all I hate myself, when, during an evening, I find myself alone in the crowd, without a dear old comrade to help me through the terrors. I try not to feel oppressed but I cannot help my feelings, whenever I gaze along one of our interminable shelves of books trailing off into the library's gray regions. Titles on books' spines can hardly be read even in adequate light. Age and the damp have faded the authors' names.

"Gin and tonic! Gin and tonic!" This abruptly from Albert in his old-fashioned horsehair chair shoved hard against a far wall. The companion pair of earless caribou heads stared vacantly down as Albert swung that retractable cane of his, rapping things and creating a fuss. Three loud raps, then: "I wonder if one of you gentlemen might bring me my Gilbey's. Jack! Is that Jack I hear? A Gilbey's and tonic with a twist. Don't sip any on the way back, Jack. I can tell when people have been drinking my drink. Jack, speak up. Where did you go?" Albert called more or less in the direction of the young man who stood only a foot or so outside the reach of Albert's red-tipped cane. As always, the blind man had heard correctly: it was Jack beside him. Albert thrashed around with the cane. Jack held back. Jack is one of those ridiculous men who wear safari outfits in town and at home. Albert chastised, "I know you're near, Jack. I *smell* you," and Jack raised a finger to his lips—playful silent warning for the rest of us to remain quiet and go along with the old

84

mischief of seeing how close you can get to Albert before he hits you with the cane.

Jack has been willing on occasion to stalk Albert for over an hour at a stretch. Everybody knows it's all in good fun. Back and forth crept Jack, keeping safe distance while waiting for the right moment to close in on Albert waving the cane feebly and begging for someone to please make his brother go away and leave him alone.

And here came Hiram rattling across the carpet toward where the action was. At Hiram's rate of travel he could expect to arrive at the porno cabinet in roughly two to four minutes, depending on variations in clearance between chairs and tables, and the speed with which other men could remove lamps and ashtrays and cachepots from the tabletops before relocating the furniture sufficiently for Hiram's walker to squeeze by as he shouted, "Where's dinner? It's time for dinner! Which of you gentlemen is in charge of our dinner?"

Who else but Jason, Joshua, and Jeremiah? Already these three were folding the napkins (Jason), counting out knives (Joshua), and polishing, with a dry cloth, the surface of the extremely long, rectangular, oak table (Jeremiah). We can't quite all fit around that table, but with enough folding card tables and petit writing desks appended at corners, and with our chairs pulled in tight or angled out just so, we can manage. No person has to feel banished to a chaise lounge, and everyone can pretty much get at the food, and no one is forced to eat off his lap. The downside is the Seating Plan in its particulars—the who-sits-next-to-whom of it all—with its impossible problems of left- and right-handed eaters placed in elbow-knocking proximity; of belligerent vegetarians always wanting to sit at a remove from meat; of equitable distribution of the red and the white wines; of the distasteful cliques—twins and young fathers come to mind—who insist on confederation to the point of pressuring others out of chairs; of old bitter hatreds and severe grain allergies and who drinks tea and who won't bear salt and how long it will take before some drunken comedian at the end of the table throws the first dinner roll. No ideal Plan has ever been devised. We would dispense with the Seating Plan altogether, but this has been tried and the outcome was not good. So the Seating Plan exists, is drawn up then drawn again, modified then reviewed, edited then erased, smudged, annotated, corrected, and drawn up one more time, in colored pencil on construction paper, by Jeremiah with his velvet-covered box of silver place cards engraved with names. You're supposed to sit where your place card tells you to sit. If you don't want to sit where your place card tells you to sit, you're supposed to inform Jeremiah, so that he can say, "Well, then, sit wherever the fuck you want."

He, Jason, and Joshua set the table(s). Jeremiah ran a tight operation. "Don't forget to fill the water pitchers. Get more ice from Clayton. Where are the pepper grinders? Those place mats, turn them around so the lion's head design is in the upper left corner. We'll put pork chops here, here, here, here, here, and here. Peas can go here, here, and over here.

Casserole here and here and there and here. Don't forget the steam trays. Give me that butter dish. There are fingerprints on it."

Then he began dealing out those engraved silver cards. A few watchers loitered nearby, restless, sipping drinks, checking to see where Jeremiah would station them, and once in a while saying to him, as he penciled in names on his color-coded Plan, "Do you think you could squeeze me in near the window for a change?" or "Can I not be next to Mongo?"

"I'll see what I can do for you," Jeremiah answered, and carried on with his business as if no one had said anything at all to him.

For my part I also like sitting near a window. You have the advantage of a breeze if things get too stuffy. The great drawback, as if this needs pointing out, is the view to the meadow and those men and women leaning together for warmth. Once or twice in the past I have chanced to look out and have seen, beyond the garden wall, a face, or so I thought, visible by firelight. But immediately the face disappeared, and whatever had seemed to me, in that instant, familiar—this disappeared as well, and I could not have told you who it was I thought I had seen, or what I had found so compelling. Probably everyone has had this kind of disconcerting experience. You spot someone in the distance, someone from the past. Someone who was once important to you. It can be shocking—recognition's unanticipated rush of confusion and expectancy. The truth is that you do not, quite often, know the person. Perhaps you've already hollered a loud

"Hello!" and instantly you feel absurd and guilty because the person is looking at you with a cautious but hopeful expression. The person, it turns out, is a stranger. So, precisely what is it that was recognized? The contour of a nose? In other words, how does the profile or posture of a stranger hold the power to summon strong and painful excitement in us? This question, applied to my current situation, might be: What is it about a view from a partly opened window that is so seductive and so frightening; and why do I therefore come to my place at the dinner table with such longing and dread? It goes without saying that my appetite for food is compromised by the terror of looking out the window.

Overhead, dim chandeliers flickered off and on at the ends of their twenty golden ropes. The long, snaking line of men to the bar was growing less long. Hiram's walker clacked across floorboards. Clacked again. It seemed to me that the walker should have worn rubber pads, to muffle sound and increase traction. Perhaps the walker had had pads once and they'd fallen off. It sounded as if Hiram was gouging the floor with a trowel. Each step brought scuffing and digging. I didn't want to say anything to Hiram about this. The soprano was singing and the dog was barking and people were trying their best under difficult circumstances to have a good time and avoid depression; and this floor has been a pitted, scraped wreck for as long as anyone can remember. Why fuss?

Hiram paused on his walker and glared in my direction. His injured hand was swollen and large. He inhaled a shallow breath. He was having trouble and his mouth was working. He said, "Doug, do you think you might grace us tonight with the costumed dance of our ancestors?"

"It's crossed my mind."

"I think I speak for all of us when I say that your performance is something we look forward to enjoying on nights like tonight."

"I'm glad to hear that, Hiram. I think it's valuable for us, as a family, to have our annual reminder of who we are and where we come from, in a cultural sense. The Corn King is as much a part of our collective history as are, well, these animals that Father shot"—waving my arm at a cheetah and a couple of denuded wildebeests, all hung in a row on the water-stained wall.

Hiram nodded and said, "I couldn't agree more, Doug. I always look forward to the winter night when you take off your clothes and put on the mask made of wood and hair."

"Yes."

"I especially like the chase through the library. What a thrill."

"It's always exciting for me, too, Hiram."

He said, "The late-night cries of strong young men take me back to my own youth. In those days we had pain and lots of it. Where did you get those flowers?"

"William."

"You should trim their stalks and put them in a vase before they turn brown and die."

"I was looking for a vase, actually."

"There's one somewhere. You'll find it," he said as he gripped the walker with his good hand; he heaved himself up, scooted the walker forward on the floor, took another labored step (onto the edge of the carpet with its knotted fringe that caught and became tangled as the walker's legs scraped past) in the direction of the oak table. He said, "I don't know about you, but I'm famished. I could eat a side of beef if I had my original teeth. Remember always to care for your teeth, Doug."

"I will."

"Do you floss? Flossing is more important than brushing, I can tell you. Too much vigorous brushing as a young man was my downfall. You scrub away the gums and before you know it the roots of your teeth are exposed to the elements and it murders you to chew, and then one after another you lose your teeth like you lose everything in life."

"I'll remember that."

"Your teeth are your greatest possession. You probably think your greatest possession is your Johnson. But it's not your johnson, it's your teeth, especially your two front teeth."

"Hmn."

"These right here," he said, opening his mouth wide to insert fingers. He touched the teeth in question, the upper incisors; he pointed these out, and when he did, when he touched these dentures, they moved. They were loose in his mouth, insecurely fastened and slipping off the gum. The effect was grotesque: Hiram's teeth hanging at an angle, wobbling in his mouth, licked by Hiram's tongue and about to fall out, as he commanded, "Stow those flowers in a vase before the petals fall off."

"Yes, sir."

Damn. Here I was again in the old unconscious complicity with Hiram's authoritarian posturing. This happens every time I engage with Hiram—it happens to a lot of us when we engage with him; we feel infantilized—and I invariably promise myself, after taking orders from Hiram, that next time I'll stand up to him, not obey, and let him get angry if he wants. Tiptoeing around Hiram's anger resolves nothing and only serves to perpetuate a strained and uneasy state of affairs in which one personality—Hiram's—overwhelmingly influences the general quality of feeling in the room as a whole. Would it be going too far to imagine my own bad moods, my terrors and despairs and so on, as personalized responses to this room-wide "Hiram-centric" emotional atmosphere? Could it then follow that Hiram is himself responsible, in large part—unwittingly, presumably—for whatever uncomfortableness we brothers experience when we congregate? Might it be possible—if, in fact, Hiram is the root cause of our squabbles and disputes (it would make sense that the first-born, Hiram, might faithfully embody the rages and pathologies of the preceding generation and, by extension, the generations before that, retreating backward in time; no single person, acting alone, is ever truly a "root cause" of inherent family dilemmas. It would be better to imagine the "root cause" as a set of psychic wounds handed down through the ages. In this way Hiram could be said to resemble that insane ancestral king about whom we know so little save that he was, as I believe I can show if I someday unearth the correct documents, our likely progenitor)—might it be possible to drive a wedge through this ancient and pervasive *household trepidation*—I don't know what else to call it—by meeting Hiram's anger with anger? It was in this absurd spirit of revolt against destiny that I now hurled the flowers to the floor before Hiram's walker, before Hiram's feet caged inside the walker's clackety aluminum framework, and said, "Find a vase yourself, you sadist."

Instantly I regretted my actions and wanted, needed, to recant and beg forgiveness.

Hiram leaned forward on his walker. He was little and bent over and liver spotted and lame, and I was startled to realize once again that I was intensely afraid of him. Throwing the flowers was nothing more than an act of self-disempowerment, an emotional demonstration of the sort that Hiram would never allow himself. Nothing I ever did seemed to have much impact on Hiram's total ability to intimidate and shame.

As for the poor lilies, scattered across the floor, they were broken; pallid white blooms had come apart on impact, and smears of pasty white pollen stained the rug in places. A few petals settled at rest around the walker's legs and on the black toes of Hiram's wing tips. Suddenly I wanted to apologize to the flowers themselves, even to William, who had brought them. I felt awful when Hiram said:

"Pick them up."

It was one of those familiar, deplorable moments. I wished for the dinner bell. No such luck yet. It wasn't time for this signal for a hundred adult men to rush from every corner of the room to grab plates and serving spoons and fight it out over the steam trays. In the meantime, there stood Denzil, and next to Denzil was Saul, and next to Saul, and more or less directly behind Hiram, were Aaron and Pierce. Here came Joe as well, tramping up from over by the porno cabinet. Joe had in his hand a broadsheet of our taboo art; and he was attempting to share this with Denzil and Saul and Aaron and Pierce; and of course there were other brothers standing around, looking on; and no one among these men wanted to get too close to a fight involving Hiram.

Hiram leaned forward over the frame of the walker, out over the metal frame. He had me in his sights. He said, "You're full of hate, aren't you, Doug?"

"No."

"You keep it all bottled up inside, your scorn and your contempt for people, and when you can't control it any longer, it comes flying out and we have one of our little tragic scenes. Isn't that right?"

"No."

"This is a family full of love, Doug. We all love one another here. This whole room is full of love. Too bad you can't feel it, Doug. You can't participate in love because you're busy tearing everybody down. You want to tear us down and you want to discredit our forefathers."

"That's not true."

"It's not enough for you to tear down the living, you have to go after the dead."

"No."

"Don't say no to me, boy. I've seen you in your same chair by the big window, night after night, rooting through the old books and papers. You think that if you find sickness in others, you'll be healthy. You think if you find weakness in others, you'll be strong. Does throwing a bunch of flowers at an old man make you feel strong, Doug?"

"No," I whispered.

"Speak louder."

"No."

"Pick up the flowers, Doug."

They were all watching me, Pierce and Aaron and Denzil and Saul and Joe with his old-fashioned erotic drawing that no one was looking at. Across the way, Jack in his safari costume stalked the blind Albert. Albert's white cane swept the air, though ineffectively. "Help me, someone. Oh, help me!" cried Albert as Jack, the expert hunter, gained on his chair.

Then the twenty chandeliers blinked off again and everything became a shade darker for an instant. It was like a negative form of lightning, perfect accompaniment to the routine thunder of wind hitting windows. Gunner barked and barked. The Doberman had managed to unsnarl his leash from the overturned art nouveau armchair, and so he was free at last and sprinting in wider and wider circles around the furniture. "Settle down, fellow," Gunners owner, Chuck, called to the racing dog.

Around and around tore Gunner with paws skittering. When the Doberman hit carpet, his claws hooked the weave for traction and the shabby fabric popped and ripped.

I prayed for Gunner to dash toward Hiram and knock him down.

Here, boy.

Instead Gunner charged between couches. Men side-stepped to avoid the onrushing dog. Gunner jumped a coffee table then disappeared into a narrow aisle of shelves housing Geology, Natural History, and Mineral Sciences. "Don't make a mess in there," Chuck called to his beloved Doberman. Could Chuck possibly have known Gunner's plans to relieve himself behind a stack of unshelved crystal spectrography manuals?

But wait. I had begun, a moment or two ago, to describe, in plain terms, the situation as it stood that night with the lilies and with Hiram—our little semipublic showdown that wasn't, in fact, so little. I always charge off the track at moments like these—the bitter moments, I guess you'd call them—and instead begin rendering the scenery and all the extraneous misbehavior of my brothers and their abysmal pets. As if anyone cares. Conflict is the really interesting

thing, I've found. Conflict! Conflict is always so difficult to
recount. By difficult I suppose I mean painful. But also I
mean demanding. The technical aspects of describing true
conflict are daunting. First, you have to establish your antag-
onists. It is important to avoid cozy oversimplifications, and
to bear down instead on all the obscure and intractable problems of identity and desire that make our lives and our needs
so various and dissimilar. The problems in describing a person are essentially problems of knowing a person. One of the
sad features of most close relationships is the decay of intimacy
as a function of time, turmoil, and all the little misunder-
standings that inevitably occur between people, leading them,
year in and year out, toward the same tired conclusions: conversation falters; friendships fail.

That said, allow me to concede that my brother Hiram is
an incredible asshole. He's just a complete jerk. He finds your
worst insecurities and then tortures you until you'll do practically anything to escape his voice's dry wheezing and the
spectacle of bony fists clutching that walker. It is true that
Hiram's voice trembles. Hiram is ninety-three, his breathing
is irregular, and his voice naturally shudders and cracks. It is
fair to guess that he may have felt, that night with flowers at
his feet and with a crowd of younger men gathered as observ-
ers, uneasy about his effectiveness as a figure of potency and
strength. He needn't have.

"Take a look at yourself, Doug. Take an honest look at
yourself standing there with your hair falling in your eyes.
You really could do with a trim and a shave." He paused,

coughed, inhaled one of his racking breaths. He resumed, "You need some new clothes. Those clothes you're wearing don't even fit you. Who wears a corduroy jacket anymore? You don't even stand straight, Doug. You slouch. You've always slouched. You have the posture of a weak person."

Times like these make me promise myself—always after the fact, of course—to skip these evenings and do something constructive instead, reacquaint myself with the more recondite heraldic literature, or sketch out, for future notation, a few pen-and-ink "family tree" line drawings. You can never have too many pristine family trees.

"Doug, it's a good thing Father isn't around anymore to see what's become of you."

Did I present such a sorrowful picture? It is true that I slouch a bit. I try not to hunch over, but I'm not getting any younger, and my shoulders ache after a wintry night sitting in a straight-backed library chair, straining my eyes over water-stained property deeds, blurry date-of-death certificates, illegibly written ships' registries. When I get up, I'm bushed and I stoop. I don't think my hair is that bad. My hair is naturally fine and growing thin on top, it's a fact, and for this reason I leave it long on the sides—just below the ears. Don't get the wrong idea. I don't wear a "comb over." There is nothing more vulgar on a mature man than a comb over. I brush my hair in the morning and, after that, pretty much let it fly where the wind blows it. My clothes, I admit, are a few seasons out of date. What about this? I've never followed fashion and I don't trust men—I'm thinking of

the twins with their colorful, expensive matching sweaters—
who heed the latest styles. It may be that this particular
outfit of mine—navy corduroy jacket with patch pockets,
my worsted wool "duck hunting" trousers with their frayed
and grimy cuffs, clothes I'm *comfortable* wearing—would
seem, to a bystander, small and rather tight, possibly even
constricting. I admit I have recently put on an inch or two
around the middle. Like I said, I'm not getting any younger.
Of course, midbody weight gain will naturally force a gar-
ment to shift. These coat sleeves could be let out. It probably
would not hurt to have a tailor cut down the lapels. I suspect that Hiram would have had less to say about my general appearance and demeanor if there had not been so
much blood—Maxwell's blood—staining my tie and shirtfront.

I said to Hiram, "The fact that I haven't shaved this week
means nothing. I only want to help. I want everyone to get
along. I want us all to be happy again."

How did this sound? Woeful? Tender? I should explain
that, in spite of antipathy toward our eldest brother, toward
his more hateful manifestations, it was still not uncommon—
and I believe this has been true for each of us in our relations
with the man—to hope for some kindness or gentleness,
even a hint of his admiration for the odd opinion or senti-
ment, whatever. You see, in his presence we felt like children,
children caught in precisely those worst moments of growing
up, those times of clear and terrifying appreciation of one's
utter smallness in the world; and this smallness is excruciat-

ing to feel in adulthood because it is a form of regression and therefore humiliating. For this reason, and in spite of mean feelings—in spite of everything—we all craved our aged brother's esteem.

He heaved himself up and gasped another painful breath. It hurt to listen to him. "Comport yourself like a man. Take full responsibility for your pernicious thoughts and immoral behavior."

Hiram could only have been referring to one thing. I believe I mentioned earlier that our brother Andrew, a sweet guy with a heart full of caring for the world's less fortunate, has lately been in the habit of passing the hat for donations to aid the itinerant people crowded in the open meadow beyond our high stone walls. The "hat" is a well-worn homburg, gray felt with narrow brim and a deep crown lined in dark material stained darker, long ago, by someone's hair oil. Into this receptacle go the bills and coins from our pockets. The hat travels from hand to hand. Wallets get opened. Andrew's take can become substantial by night's end.

Once in a while, the hat of money will rest on a table. Someone might set it down, and it might then be overlooked for an instant if something diverting is happening elsewhere, a quarrel breaking out or Gregory solemnly lighting one of his splendid, cognac-drenched, flaming desserts.

Let's just say for now that I know exactly the amount that I have borrowed—over time—from the hat, and that it is only just roughly less than eight hundred dollars.

"I've been short on cash lately! What's the big deal? I'm going to pay it back!" I cried at Hiram.

To underscore the point, and to further illustrate the essential humility of my character, I walked forward two steps and, abruptly, dramatically, as if swooning, collapsed before Hiram's feet. I dropped to my hands and knees and reached out for those broken lilies. As I have, I believe, already observed, several pale blooms had come to rest directly atop Hiram's large black wing-tip shoes. This banal but evocative white-on-black color symbolism was not lost on me as I plucked up one, then another and another ruined flower. Human beings in stressful relationships will frequently behave in ways that contradict or even reverse their own most certain expectations. The fact remained that I had, in a moment of pride, demolished a gift bouquet. I recollect this now, not to defend my sorrowful deeds, my kneeling, my submission, that night before Hiram, but to articulate a postulate: once an authentic conflict reaches its climax, then time will seem suddenly interrupted and the adrenaline will flow in your blood and your head will feel hot and cold at the same moment, because you've got to choose the upright thing to do. I believe that the patriarchal succession leaves in its wake a readable trail—clues to the formation of character and personality—as generation after generation adapts to the pain and suffering of family life.

The first Doug on record in the New World died during birth, in the backcountry, in 1729.

Another Doug, a cousin of the first, was by all accounts an

intelligent and sensitive child, but was thrown from a horse and killed at an early age.

The next Doug reached puberty before succumbing to injuries sustained in a plummet from a roof.

That Doug's nephew and namesake was lost at age five in a boating accident on the black river that snakes through the mountains to the west.

After that there were no more Dougs for a while. In 1854, one materializes among the rolls of a preparatory academy run by a Scotsman who believed in the godliness of child labor and freezing baths. Need I say more? In the decades that followed, the name Doug became identified with an array of superstitions and death anxieties.

This brings me to the situation as it stood that night in the red library with Hiram and those flowers. How could I, a fully grown Doug descended from a worthy line in which previous Dougs were squandered so beautifully before their primes, forgo this chance to establish a magnificent and honorable behavioral precedent, a fine example for all my brothers and for any Doug who might one day thrill to call me his ancestor? I do not consider my prostration before Hiram a surrender. Not in the least. Kneeling down for flowers was a triumphal revelation of willingness to quit a meaningless standoff in favor of community and concord. It felt good to get on the floor.

The carpet was obscenely dirty. Who was responsible for vacuuming? I looked underneath claw-footed chairs and saw dust balls, ripped papers, desiccated food particles and

cigarette butts, matches burnt black, and many gray heaps
that must've been ashes surreptitiously dumped. The carpet
itself was gritty to the touch; the weave felt suffused with sand
and dirt, and the rancid smell that rose from it was of something wet and dead. How many after-dinner ports had been
absently tipped and allowed to dribble into sugary pools that
fed the bugs and soaked through these old threads, down into
the foam matting and between cracks dividing floorboards
that groaned beneath our shoes and boots all stomping this
way and that, to the bathroom, the porno cabinet, the drinks
table?

Hiram's stockings were checkered and sheer. One had
slid down its leg. There was not much leg there. The skin
was chalky alabaster, speckled brown. Hiram's trousers rode
high on him. He belted these at the bottom of his rib cage.
If you look around the world, you'll notice elderly men
wearing pants in this fashion. Hiram's were green and a
mismatch with his socks. The shoes, as I have said, were
black, and they were massive. They held my attention. I
should say that they held me under their spell. I reached out
to take a flower that lay across a shoe's toe. As if responding,
this shoe moved toward my hand. Of course, this was only
Hiram shifting his foot. But it seemed to me, down there on
my belly on the reeking carpet, as though this fat black wing
tip had become self-activated, that it had decided, all by itself, to proffer its white bloom. Obviously, Hiram's wing tip
was not alive. I knew this. It's just that the shoe looked so *big*
up close, and so oblong, so impressively thick-skinned, with

its laces like whiskers and its toe that glistened like an animal's wet nose.

I wanted to pet it.

Perhaps, if I caressed the shoe, I might like myself better. I have found it calming, from time to time, to make a small gesture expressing abjection, and to really get in touch with feelings of loneliness and shame.

I crawled toward the shoe. It was Hiram's right shoe, not the left. It rested beside its mate inside the open metal cage formed by the walker's tubular framework. The shoe was a foot away from me. I was flat on my stomach. One dozen broken lilies were in my hands. These flowers were barely more than denuded stems. The stems were bent and their fallen petals lay scattered across the carpet. I inched forward. I suppose you could say I was sneaking up on Hiram's shoe. I dragged myself along; I stayed low; I tracked my quarry. The carpet's rank musk smelled delicious. I breathed in the smell. The shoe waited. It seemed to regard me. Tiny impressions punched in the uppers made lacy, delicate arabesques, heavenly swirls in the black leather.

Such thick soles.

I crawled closer—near enough to kiss the shoe, almost. My breath fogged its shine. Light dust showed on its toe. Suddenly Hiram's foot inside the shoe moved and I feared for an instant that I had charged too close too fast and would frighten the shoe away. But the shoe stayed put. Its movement was slight—only Hiram stretching, redistributing his weight, getting comfortable. Naturally, Hiram's slightly moving foot caused the shoe's uppers to stretch and expand (much in the manner of a languid animal's leathery back, whenever the animal shifts its weight or stretches after a nap), and this movement, the shoe's breathy dilation, seemed to me so absolutely lifelike—and of course it was; Hiram's old foot was alive and kicking, as they say—so adorable and beguiling, so downright friendly, that I began to feel warm all over. I felt happy. I felt, in my happiness, able to do what I had crawled across the unclean floor to do: I dropped the lilies, reached out, and stroked, with my hand, Hiram's wing tip.

It seemed to like this. I gave it a squeeze. I felt Hiram's foot buried inside. The foot made subtle nuzzling motions, as if responding to my touch. And with each soft nuzzle from the shoe, I felt an accompanying wave—these were physical sensations that originated deep in my stomach—of pleasure. I became aware of a wonderful feeling of peacefulness and ease that I can describe only as a general loosening of bodily tensions. The miniature waves of pleasure feathered out along my arms and legs, and I noticed in myself a capacity for deeper breathing; each exhalation of rotten air became a gentle evacuation of the stresses and strains of life. How relaxing it was to lie down on the floor. In my right hand was Hiram's black shoe. Here were Hiram's trouser legs, and here were the walker's slender posts. Lily petals resembled water flowers drifting across the dark and tranquil rug. Cigarette ashes rose up beside chair legs; the ash piles looked to me like volcanoes. Convoys of brothers' feet passed in every direction. I could see every type of foot-wear, loafers and canvas sneakers, lace-up oxfords and water-resistant work boots, expensive running shoes and cowboy and riding boots and moccasins and floppy bedroom slippers, sandals worn with socks, you name it, dozens of shoes stamping to and fro; and I could feel, as I lay breathing deeply on our threadbare carpet, the mingled repercussions of everyone's steps, the mild shock waves echoing through the floor and the rug.

What a sweet feeling. It was a vibrating massage. I breathed out, let myself go slack, and considered, for the moment, the other men lying on the floor.

The doctor was closest. His head was purple and his eyes stared from swollen sockets. One might imagine that the rumbling made by his brothers' feet produced a gentle back rub, relieving Barry's aches.

A few steps past Barry was Virgil. Virgil was curled tight around his embroidered cushion. He trembled; you could see his shoulders twitch, but this was, as I may have mentioned, often the case when he slept. The trembling did not appear violent. Clearly our resonating floor had soothed Virgil.

Likewise with Max. Max was still on his back; his nose no longer bled; he seemed looser in the body. Evidently the floorboards were helping him to unwind.

It is worth noting this phenomenon—in which a lot of thoughtless pacing around the room produced a desirable secondary outcome, healing body massage—as an instance of spontaneous, intrafamilial mutuality and caring. No doubt this kind of unpremeditated caretaking occurs frequently in large communities, perhaps even within other species with complex societies, like the termites and bees. It pleased me enormously to imagine my brothers going about routine business while serendipitously tending to one another's health and well-being. This is the way family members ought to coexist. I can honestly declare that, in that moment, belly-down on our floor, gazing at the ashes, the injured men, the promenading shoes, in that moment I loved my brothers.

I gave another firm squeeze to Hiram's wing tip, then crept closer and snuggled. Gently I rested my cheek on the shoe's cold toe. I could feel, pressed sharply against my chest, the hypodermic syringes and assorted medicine vials in my jacket's inside breast pocket. I did not mind the pain of lying on these things. On the contrary, the needles were a comfort to me. Tremors rolled through the floor, and I heard Gunner the Doberman barking from the dark canyons of bookshelves. The shoe felt so comfortable to lie on. Its smell of leather and pungent black polish gave me a memory that I could not place—the inexplicit memory of a feeling that was like sadness, though not exactly sadness. Certain feelings lie in wait for certain sounds or scents to activate them. Everyone knows the power of the senses. Deep memories of feelings describe the earliest manifestations of the Self. Pillowed by Hiram's shoe, smelling its leather, I felt transported back to a time too distant to accurately recollect. I felt with real conviction that I was alone in the world, that my brothers were not gathered around me, that no people were outside in the meadow beyond our garden wall. I imagined our garden full of green trees and youthful, blooming plants. The rose garden, in particular, appeared, in my mind, splendid with color. I suppose it was Hiram's shoes themselves, and his shoe polish with its fertile, earthy smell, that provoked these images of red flowers, crawling vines, branches swaying in a breeze.

"Doug."

My eyes were closed. I did not want to open them.

"Doug."

A draft coming in the window made me cold and I shivered. The floor felt cold.

"Doug. Look at me. Doug," the voice said. And I could hear the dog again, barking. The dog sounded frightened and far away. He could just as easily have been close. I felt a hand touch my shoulder, and I looked up and saw that it was Spooner leaning over me, gazing down toward me. His face wore a troubled expression. He spoke into my ear. "Let go of Hiram's foot."

"Spooner, it's you. Thank God. Give me a drink, man. Please, give me a drink."

Then Hiram's shoe kicked and squirmed. I held on but the shoe kicked my face, and Hiram exclaimed, "Get him off me! He's a dangerous person!"

"Hang on a minute, Hiram," Spooner said, and saying this, he knelt on the floor beside me; he reached out, closed his hand around my wrist, and began gently tugging me away. "Doug, you can't be grabbing people's feet. It's not right."

"Give me a drink, Spooner. Come on, man. I know you've got some on you."

"I don't know if that's a good idea, Doug." He gave my wrist a yank but I was holding on tight. "You know what happens when you drink," he said, straining hard against me.

"Nothing's going to happen. I just want a taste. Nothing's going to happen."

"That's what you always say, Doug."

"I mean it."

He seemed to consider this. "If I give you a taste, will you let go of Hiram's foot?"

"Yes."

"Promise?"

"Yes."

He stopped tugging. He released my hand and reached into his inside coat pocket. That's where he carries his handsome pewter flask filled with cognac. I felt so happy when I saw Spooner's flask. He keeps this with him at all times. It is as if the flask is a part of the man. It wears a cork stopper secured inside a glass cap appended from a delicate, silver hinge. It holds a half-pint. It's antique.

"Pull him off me! Hurry up down there! I want my dinner!" Hiram's voice commanded. I was aware, now, of other brothers looking on, clean shirt collars and their shaved faces luminous beneath dim chandelier light. I could make out Pierce and Jacob, Allan and Ralph, Nick and Saul, and, a little ways off, directly behind Hiram's walker, Joe, holding, at his side, that eighteenth-century French erotic drawing on brown paper.

"Just a taste, Doug," Spooner said.

"Only a taste," I agreed. My face where Hiram's shoe had kicked me felt sore. I had numbness and tingling around one eye. The hypodermic needles in my pocket were biting into my chest. I heard a voice in the crowd explaining the situation to someone. "He's locked onto Hiram's foot. He won't let go." And another voice said, "He got hold of me like that once. I was wearing hiking shoes. Doug got tangled up in the laces and I couldn't shake him. It was terrible." This second voice went on to report other details. I did not pay strict attention. The pewter flask had made its appearance from Spooner's coat and Spooner was unscrewing its glass top and pulling the cork all in one artful motion. Would it be going too far to say that this was what I had been waiting for since nightfall? To nurse from my brother's flask!—here was a happiness in life. I took the metal spout in my mouth and sucked hard at it, the way a young calf sucks, to feel safe in his world and warm inside himself, and to become strong.

I got a fair swallow considering the size of the spout and was therefore pleased with myself.

"Pick him up, gentlemen," Spooner said to those standing closest, and I felt arms around me and men's hands clasping my arms and then the spout went away as I was hoisted from the rug. A bell was ringing in the distance. This was the dinner bell. After standing, I surprised my brother Ralph with a hug for helping me. There was a general movement toward the oak table, and merely by standing erect I seemed to become swept up in this movement, brothers making their way to seats. Of course it was late and everyone had had a lot to drink and nothing to eat but peanuts. For this reason there was a fair amount of swaying from side to side as men smelled food rolling in through the library's northern doors, on trolleys pushed by Jason and Joshua. Up ahead, over the horizon of swaying heads, fortunate brothers arrived at the oak table and stationed water glasses in preferred places, or draped jackets casually on chair backs to claim spots not named as theirs on Jeremiah's seating plan. Brothers in the rear had to step over Virgil to get in line. Feet shuffled and the floorboards groaned and groaned. No one was talking in that solemn progression that advanced over Virgil. Several men were smoking, and at intervals along our line small clouds of cigarette smoke drifted or were blown upward out of mouths toward the ceiling.

Now it turned out that Donovan, while I had been resting, had kindled the fire in the hearth. His blaze was really up. Dry logs were catching, the flue was drawing, and everything seemed grand except for the fact that bats tenant the chimney. This was not a new problem. It never fazed anyone particularly when three or five bats flapped out of the hearth and turned figure eights around the chandelier cords above our heads. We keep nets on long poles expressly for this event.

That night it was the triplets, Herbert, Patrick, and Jeffrey, who grabbed nets on poles and went hunting bats. The triplets are professionally trained dancers, so they can do this sort of thing.

"Pork chops for dinner," I said quietly to the back of the man in front of me. This was Rex. He answered gruffly, "Nothing ever changes around here, does it?" and I asked him if he had by any chance noticed Spooner in the crowd. He told me he hadn't. He then said, "Stop bumping into me, Doug." I hadn't realized I had been and I apologized and moved away. Milton, Pierce, and Fielding were strolling along in a clique behind me. I asked if they'd noticed Spooner anywhere, but no one had. Fielding was carrying his broken camera's parts in his hands. A triplet shouting, "Heads up!" raced by, enormous net trailing, after a bat that apparently had touched down on the underside of an elk's antler. Everyone turned to watch, but when the triplet arrived at the elk, the bat had flown. Milton said, "That was Patrick."

"It was Jeffrey," Pierce said.

"No," said Milton. "It was Patrick."

"Jeffrey."

"Patrick."

"I don't know how you can think such a wrong thing. That was obviously Jeffrey," said Pierce.

"Bet?"

"Bet."

"It might have been Herbert," suggested Fielding, who

was awkwardly trying, as he walked, to join his fractured movie camera's pieces together in his hands.

"That wasn't Herbert," said Pierce, and he went on to explain, "Herbert's fat."

Silence followed this. After a moment Fielding announced, "Well, they're all fat."

"They quit dancing," I chipped in. "One of them injured his knee and they all retired, the idiots."

There was silence again. We were approaching the dinner table, but a crowd blocked the way. Some had sat and others were milling around with their water glasses. I could see Zachary ahead and made a mental note to stay away from him. Jason and Joshua were striking matches, igniting flames underneath food trays. Fielding said, "I've got twenty that says that was Herbert. We'll each put in twenty and winner takes all."

Milton said to Fielding, "You might as well hand over that cash right now, Brother, because I can feel the vibrations around people and my feelings say that was Patrick."

Milton then said to me, "Doug, you want in on this?" and Fielding said, "Doug can't be in on this, Milton. We've got three wagers on three men. What is Doug going to do, bet on Herbert *and* Patrick?"

"Oh, yes. You're right."

Fielding suggested, "Doug can hold the pot. Is that all right with you, Doug?"

"Sure."

"Everyone give Doug twenty dollars."

In this way I came into a modest short-term loan. I tucked the money into my billfold for safekeeping. By then we had made it, our little group, to the oak table and dinner, and so it was time for us to go separate directions in search of assigned seats. What I mean is that Milton, Pierce, and Fielding all went one way, while I headed another through the crowd.

This then was that part of the evening when we all came together as a family at last around one table.

As always before dinner, Jeremiah was directing traffic and losing his patience when people neglected to sit, or refused to sit, where the seating chart required.

The chart is color-coded on construction paper, three feet by four feet unrolled, eraser-streaked, specific. Hiram goes at the table's head. This is a particular that never varies—Hiram's inked in—because who would dare steal this man's place? According to the chart, Hiram sits with his back to the rose window, in a wooden chair that resembles—what else—a throne. Hiram, eating dinner, looks tiny in his oversize chair; all that is visible of him is the crown of his head and speckled hands reaching up from below the table's edge to grasp cutlery. Fortunately, Donovan's place is on Hiram's left. Donovan carves the old man's vegetables into squares and manually helps Hiram lift fork to mouth. This is moving and dispiriting to watch. The table's corner, directly to the left of Donovan, is where Lester belongs. Lester and

Donovan look alike and celebrate the same birthday, though Donovan is the older of the two by several years. Lester keeps Donovan company while Donovan slices food for Hiram. These men are old pals. Around the corner from them, at the first setting along the oak table's protracted straightaway, is their brother Porter. Following Porter on the seating chart are Chuck, Henry, Drake, Eric, and Phil. All these names are written in lemon yellow pencil. After that it's downhill for many chairs. Frank, Noah, Jim, Vaughan, Dennis, Tom, and a few others occupy a blue-designated "quiet zone" in which nobody talks except to request salt or the potatoes. The quiet zone was founded long ago, by Jim, who at some point decided that our dinner hour had become so clamorous he couldn't stand it. It goes without saying that they get a lot of grief, these quiet eaters, from across the table. First on Hiram's right comes Richard. Hiram likes Richard and Richard is fond of Hiram; both are sufferers in the body, and maybe that's the reason; Richard, as I think I have mentioned, has that neurological problem. Who cares to watch his head bob wildly as he raises his glass to drink? Seamus is often asleep and probably that is why Jeremiah seats him next to the jiggling man. Seamus and Hiram reminisce about long-ago football glories whenever Seamus is not dozing in his chair. Around this right-hand corner, then, comes a gang of buddies all in a line. Ralph, Nick, Allan, Jacob, Aaron, and Raymond sit together, have sat together, in the same seats, for as long as anyone remembers. They're polite as a rule, though they raise their voices when the talk turns to money. After this group come rowdies who drink far too much red wine and make loud trouble for the quiet zone opposite. Everyone agrees Topper, Temple, Denzil, Fish, and Mongo should be relocated, but for reasons of his own Jeremiah won't approve. Dining next to Mongo is Simon, who hates every minute. Jonathan's chair is beside Simon's. Next the chart shows, in bold red crayon, a three-man "medical" block consisting of Anton, Irving, and our physician, Barry. Anton is chronically depressed, and Irv takes clozapine to inhibit visual and auditory hallucinations of marauding hordes of men storming across an open meadow to personally attack and crush him. Barry runs frequent blood tests on both men; he likes to keep an eye on their diets, and that is the principal reason these three sit next to the left-handed vegetarians— Foster, Andrew, Eli, Milton, Pierce, Fielding—one after another marked off in green pencil down the table. Straight across from the vegetarians is a seat that remains empty. This is George's. If George ever shows up for dinner, he'll have his old place, no question. Twins come after George, one set only, Michael and Abraham. Jeremiah objects to overlarge cliques— they create dead spots and really bring a table down—and he already graciously allows Jim's quiet zone. Certain young fathers—Clay, Seth, Vidal, Gustavus, Joe—follow the twins. These men are discouraged from reading pornography at mealtime, but as a rule Joe pilfers something lewd and beautiful from the glass cabinet, spreads this on the oak table. This offends Winston and Charles. Fights break out. The fights are rarely physical. Winston and Charles are always calmed from across the table by their brothers Lawrence and Peter. After Winston and Charles comes Vincent, and after Vincent comes Paul, then Russel, then Spencer, then Sergio. Sergio is a good talker; he keeps the ball rolling. Across on the right-hand side of the table, it's Christopher, Stephen, Siegfried—these three truly enjoy one another's company— followed down the line by two more young fathers, Brice and Dutch, and next to Dutch, written in bright, bright orange—I've never figured out the logic behind this—yours truly. It's a dismal state of affairs all around. On my right I'm joined by Jack in his safari costume. It gets worse. To Jack's immediate right, two seats down from me, we find the last twins, Scott and Samuel, and after these comes Kevin. What this means is that there is no one to chat with and dinner is a chore, and there is no point looking across the table for company, because here's who's there: Rex, Mr. Gruff; Bertram, Mr. Nosebleeds; Walter, Mr. Wattled Boar. Next of course comes unhappy Virgil, who dislikes Walter as much as I do. Max at least makes interesting conversation. He sits far away at the end of the table, but he and I can sometimes manage a dialogue if we shout over the heads of Kevin and Angus and the others crowded near the corner. It's always a hardship when Max can't make it for dinner. On those occasions Zachary gets plenty of extra elbow room at his place beside Maxwell's chair. In fact there is no good seat for Zachary. He picks on everyone and no one is safe. Bob can at least check Zachary's reaching around to steal leftovers from Albert's plate. It's a lucky thing for Albert that he is adapted to his condition, that he experiences his blindness more as a trial than a deprivation. The sightless man is quite unlike Hiram, who lives with a body that will hardly cooperate with the simplest desires for comfort and mobility. It is true that there is dignity in the freedom to act in a material way upon one's world. Hiram's predictable violence is, in part, his expression of former volition. I think we all understand this.

Far down the table, down the long ranks of men facing each other, past the quiet zone and the vocal womanizers and the left-handed vegetarians, down between Bob and Albert at the foot of the oak table, far from Hiram and with an unobstructed view of glowing candelabra and steaming food trays, of silver spoons and our flushed faces beneath the radiant purple window that seems to float up in darkness behind Hiram's wooden throne—down here, viewing all this and more from the foot of our extraordinarily lengthy table, from its other head, is our Benedict.

Some nights Benedict will bring a bit of "work" from his entomology laboratory, a living specimen, or, if we're blessed, several, sealed in a dish. Brothers gather around to hear Benedict describe the pellucid egg sac depending from the thorax of a black beetle that displays horns and an armored casing harder and more resilient than our very own bone-china demitasse cups. If we're really lucky, Benedict will arrange his beetles on the table and they'll sprint from place setting to place setting. Occasionally bets are taken, favorite beetles named, finish lines drawn with mayonnaise. You wouldn't think a bug race could be so exciting. Frequently a beetle will detour, climb into someone's soup, and kick around awhile before drowning. This can be a tension breaker on nights when we brothers are not getting along. It's always some twin who shouts, "Benedict, take your roaches off the table! They're covered with germs!"

Benedict will explain, patiently, that his beetles are clean, and that roaches and humans are diseased.

"The sooner everyone sits, the sooner we'll enjoy our first course!"

This was Jeremiah screaming at us. No one paid him much attention. Why did he bother? Mobs have a way of not hearing, and we were no exception. It was impossible in the confusion to avoid knocking into people. "Sorry, sorry," I apologized as I shouldered my way to the sideboard. To get through to the plates I leaned against Jonathan's back and pushed hard. This man stumbled forward, complaining, "Don't shove."

I lied, "I'm not shoving! Someone is pushing me! It's a pack of animals in here!" The lights flickered off and stayed off. Everyone ceased moving, briefly, while waiting for our twenty rusted chandeliers to blink on again. During this interlude of calm I gave Jonathan's back a sudden, severe body block. I did not see where he fell.

The lights were restored and I arrived at the plates well ahead of most others.

"Doug," a voice near me called. I pretended not to hear

and headed instead toward the oak table and our pork chops heaped in trays. Multitudes, it seemed, had conceived this idea. It wasn't simply a question of waiting in line. There were no lines, only dense, swarming formations around the food.

In situations like this, my football experience can come in handy.

I tucked my warm, empty plate securely under my arm, extended my other arm in front of me—locked at the elbow for ramming strength—put my head down, and rushed forward into the assembly.

The first person I hit was Raymond. He was turned away from me, and I took full advantage with a stiff-arm blow to the rib cage. This knocked the wind from his lungs and Raymond's plate from his hands. The crashing plate drew attention and I was able to sidestep quickly between Topper and Vince. I had to go low and almost sacrificed my balance but fortunately came up against Paul and used him as a backstop. Paul held on to his plate but fell away against Dennis, and that left a clear path with no visible obstructions except Albert and Mongo. It is my feeling that you can't tackle a blind man. And Mongo is too big for me to hit effectively, though he is slow. I ran toward him, a straight-on course, like open-field running, then at the last second feinted hard to the left, dodging him. It felt good, very good, to give Mongo the fake. I believed at this point that I was unimpeded. I hadn't counted on Richard. Richard stepped out from behind Michael and Abraham. He got directly between me and the food. His head was shaking, up and down, up and down, the way it does. I wanted to hit him. If I did, I might be chastised for running over a person who has nerve damage. I ran in place while considering what to do. I could smell the pork chops and their aroma was superb. I decided that Richard was, after all, a man, and could weather blows. I inhaled a deep breath and charged in hard with an elbow aimed low at his kidneys. However, I lost my balance and this time saw no alternative but to take the dive. I was less than five yards short of the table. It had been a good forward rush and I felt all right.

"Doug."

It was the voice from over near the sideboard. It was Seamus's voice. He was awake. He said, "Nicely run, Doug. You took a nasty spill but you kept possession of your plate. That's the kind of spirit that wins games." He offered me his large hand. "It's good to see you getting in some practice for Sunday's game against the Episcopal Ministers."

"We can beat those guys," I said. Seamus observed, "That's one serious carpet burn you've got there, Doug. I hope that's not your throwing arm."

He was right. My forearm was red from my fall. This wasn't, luckily, my throwing arm. As soon as I became aware of its redness, I felt pain.

"How did you hurt your face, Doug? You look like you're going to have a shiner around that eye. You didn't smack a chair, did you?"

"I got kicked."

"Bad luck," said Seamus. "Who kicked you? We'll get him on the team."

"Hiram."

"Hmn. Hiram was an excellent ball carrier at one time, but he's too frail for contact sports now." These words were followed by silence between us, respectful contemplation of the sage man's gridiron days, I suppose. Finally Seamus announced, "We're all going to grow old and die."

Why bring this up at dinner? I asked my brother, "Do you feel you've lived a good life so far? I mean, if your time came, if you had a terminal illness, or fell from a height, do you think you would feel proud of the things you've said and done?"

"Yes," he announced, then appeared to deliberate. "And also no. Kind of yes and no. Same as everybody."

I stayed quiet. After another moment Seamus said something I could not make out above raucous dining noises. This racket of men eating was made louder by the acoustic properties of the room. The high ceiling vaults throw echoes in every direction. It can be difficult, when forks and knives are ringing out against plates, to determine direction and proximity of sounds, especially voices, which seem to bubble up for an instant, excitedly declare something unqualified by any context—"I know everything there is to know about the rotator cuff!" I heard one exclaim, and another asked, "Seriously, though, what did Maxwell mean when he said, 'The God is above us'?"—then recede again into the muddle and roar, our party in full swing.

"Did you hear that?" I asked Seamus.

"What?" the man asked.

"That echo?"

We listened, but the sound—it was the hushed noise of someone crying, softly, softly—had faded. Seamus said, "See if you can get in three sets of twenty wind sprints before Sunday's game, Doug."

"Will do."

I wanted to hear the crying again. That sound didn't come back. A black bat darted quickly through the air over the oak table, pursued to table's edge by a triplet lunging over place mats with his net. People weren't sitting in their assigned seats. The Doberman barked again—he'd emerged from the stacks and was pacing anxiously around chairs. Apparently he'd spied the bat. A voice in the crowd suggested opening windows for the bat, or bats, to fly out of. Brothers put down plates and went to do this. Several tall windows were painted shut, but most were not. One near the head of the table was unlatched, then raised, with difficulty, by Brice. He had to struggle to budge it. The window sash was warped; going up, rotted wood scraped in the ancient frame. Other windows went up in the same rough way, and winds swept into the library. The winds blew manuscript pages from a table near the African masks. These papers sailed up into the room, and the dog, excited, saw them and ran in circles, around and around below soaring white sheets, eyeing them as they drifted, huge confetti fluttering down, page after page settling around Gunner on the floor.

It was that time of evening when things start going wrong and it's every man for himself.

"Dinner's getting cold!" Jeremiah shouted at the men raising windows. The dog, smelling meat, left papers on the ground and trotted, head up, across the room to our table.

"Leash that animal!" someone shouted in the direction of Chuck's assigned seat. This chair was unoccupied because Chuck had taken himself and a bottle of Scotch off to a corner table shared by Leon, Bennet, and Saul.

Displaced brothers roamed at large. The twins were assembled, predictably, in their line of eight. Clay, Seth, Vidal, Gustavus, and Joe had been orphaned from their seats. Young Jeremy's place was free; this boy remained on his back on the purple divan, eyes closed, recovering from Fielding's assault earlier in the night. That fight seemed, to me, like something that had happened ages before. But it had been a recent event. What time was it anyway? I didn't dare ask. As I believe I've mentioned, a question like that can start a brawl. Seth and Vidal hurriedly ran around the foot of the dinner table, grabbed the chairs left vacant by Samuel and Scott. The triplets, off chasing bats, lost their places to Ralph, Lewis, and Rod. Noises everywhere were getting louder. Gunner the Doberman's eyes glistened, watery. Frank looked unhappy. Our pork chops were disappearing fast. A man's voice beside me said, "It's past ten o'clock."

I'd not realized I had asked. Surely in all this chaos it would be easy to speak out unknowingly, to utter, in an offhand way, one's thoughts—and be overheard. I said, "Oh, we always eat so late," and watched uprooted men race frantically around the oak table, this way and that like competitors playing musical chairs. Many carried plates.

Periodically, one would say, "You're in my seat," or, "Pardon me, is this chair taken?"

One after another, the roving men dropped into places. Joshua with his long kitchen matches leaned across the table at its middle—squeezing, sideways, between Foster and Andrew—to light candles. Wine carafes traveled from hand to hand until drained. You could tell which men were already finishing second or third glasses. They were the most voluble. They wore inscrutable, wide smiles on blushing faces, and their voices, when shouting greetings down the great length of the table, rang out ecstatically. "I love you, man! You're my brother!" Lewis hollered to Denzil, and Denzil, returning that toast, cried, "You're my brother, too, and I love you like one!"

Meanwhile the dog paced behind chairs, excited and hungry. "Here, doggy," a voice called, and before anyone could object, a pork chop was hurled through the air at Gunner. The chop flew upward in a spiraling arc, up into the high darkness and out of sight above the chandeliers, then straight back into vision as it fell into the light at Gunner's feet and landed with a plop on the rug where the dog seized it between wet teeth.

Practically everybody was eating. The menu was braised pork chops, peas (not canned peas), scalloped potatoes in a dill sauce, a delightful squash-and-eggplant casserole, wild rice for the vegetarians, dinner rolls in those foil trays, and a lettuce and cucumber salad. Dessert was a surprise and I was hoping as always for coconut cake. I'd not yet loaded my plate. Someone at the table struck his glass with a knife blade, and this meant time for before-dinner announcements.

Ping. Ping.

Brothers looked up from plates. Kevin put down his glass and the butter knife he'd rapped it with and began, "I have a brief announcement. Can I have your attention? Excuse me? I'd like to make an announcement? There will be a meeting tonight after supper, of brothers concerned about water damage and falling plaster in the library. As some of you may know, a slow drip, directly over Philosophy of Mind, has recently waterlogged and destroyed seventy to eighty percent of Cognitive Theory. Additional roof leaks are causing runoff and resultant buckling along many stretches of wall, as well as structural deterioration throughout the ceiling. We can expect worse with snow, which, I might add, is predicted for later this evening."

He sat. There was audible mumbling up and down the table's length. The loss of Cognitive Theory was news to me. Another knife pealed against another wineglass, and it was Andrew speaking this time. He stood at his place among the left-handed vegetarians and said, "Some of us got talking a while ago and decided the best thing we could do with the money we've raised for the people in the meadow is invest it. We're currently exploring high-yield bond issues and longer-term fund packages that offer security and growth. If the market remains vigorous and donations continue at the present rate, we could be managing a very solid trust within, say, five to seven years. This will allow us to assist the needy without depleting capital."

Assenting nods followed. "Good idea" and "That's thinking, Andrew" were typical comments.

Next it was Henry's turn. Henry got up and said, "I will set up chessboards in the usual place by Sociology and Urban Studies and regular players can have their coffee there if they want, since it is getting late. Just a note for any new players who might be interested in the ancient, manly game of chess. As some of you already know, our brother Paul has been on a lucky streak"—knowing laughter at this from several chess players—"and we very much need some genius to come around and knock him off the top of the ladder. A couple of tips. Don't waste the clock, and think twice before trading queens because Paul's endgame is hard to beat. Anyone interested in trying is more than welcome."

"No one will beat me!" boasted Paul, and the chess players laughed again, and then Frank stood at his place and said, "I don't think I could beat Paul at chess, but I'll gladly take his money at poker." This naturally brought on more laughter from different locations around the table. It felt good to hear all this laughing. Frank went on amiably, "We'll ask those of you sitting at the smaller tables to please bus your plates after dinner and get the hell out of the way so we serious gamblers can get down to business."

"Fuck off!" shouted a voice from one of these tables. It was Chuck, apparently well into his Scotch. It was not clear whether Chuck intended humor. Chuck's exclamation had an aggressive, uncomfortable, borderline quality. The man had a problem with alcohol. Someone should help him. Frank, tight himself, wisely elected to avoid trouble with a fellow drunk. Frank chuckled, "Ha ha," and sat quickly in his chair.

After Frank's announcement came Tom's, also about some game or other. More announcements followed Tom's, and these as well were about games: dice, baseball, hearts, our usual pastimes, and also one I'd never heard of called ground war, canceled due to the harsh weather outdoors. Finally it was Seamus's turn to speak. He'd gotten his food and made it, against great odds, all the way to his seat, far off near the head of the table. He stood up and—sleepily, I thought, or drunkenly; he was weaving from side to side—mumbled, "Listen up. Half-hour shirts-versus-skins play drill. Later tonight. Damn those bats. Cold in here. So cold. Football players huddle together for calisthenics at the black sofa after dessert and coffee. Oh."

He collapsed backward into his seat. Seamus's head drooped forward and he sank down, as if dragged over by its weight, and fell easily asleep, passed out with his head resting on the table. No one spoke.

After a brief time Seamus lifted his head and appeared to gaze around. He pushed back his chair, got up, walked slowly off into the stacks.

I seized this moment of wordless silence to make my own announcement. Let me say right now that my message to my brothers was entirely unplanned, yet completely heartfelt, and, I might add, important for them to hear. Before speaking, I waited for Seamus to disappear into Poems and Plays of the Restoration. Once he was safely out of sight I cleared my throat; I stood straight (shoulders loose so that air could fill my chest), relaxed my diaphragm—reminding myself not to hyperventilate while talking—and said, "Genealogy is more than a system for cataloging descent. The genealogical tree is a living organism. It is a living, breathing tree, and the limbs of this tree are human lives, hardier than any wood. The bonds joining lives, life after life, reach across time. And human bonds are always emotional creations. The student of human births and deaths will experience, perhaps as a distant and unaccountable memory, the traces of very old affections, all the joys and disappointments that have forever bound people together in families. Who has ever visited a grave site; who has lingered in that silence among graves and not felt a chill travel down the spine? Am I alone among my brothers in these sympathies for the perished?"

I felt overcome with tiredness. I could hear the dog's teeth gnawing gristle and bone. Cold air swept into the room and I felt a chill. I was thinking fondly of other Dougs, those dead in infancy and their childhoods, and unborn Dougs to come. Would it be going too far to imagine past souls contained within my own, my old soul spirited through life, again and again, within the happy succession of men called Doug?

I pressed on with my impromptu lecture to my brothers. It was clear to me, from the way their faces gazed up at mine, that I held their attention. I'm not a bad speaker, once I get rolling. I bore down and made eye contact with men in their seats, man after man, to give each the impression that I was addressing *him,* in a personal, confidential way; to make all my brothers stop chewing, put down their forks, and show some manners. "The dead should not be feared. Their spirits are inside us. The dead inhabit us. I feel the spirits of ancestors alive in me. The dance of the Corn King is the nocturnal dance of death and the life that grows out of death! Cold winds of the coming winter blow through the red library! Winter is upon us! Who will take up the knife and cut out the living, beating heart of the Corn King? The Corn King must be sacrificed!"

No one moved. One after another, my beloved brothers turned away from me. They fidgeted in their seats, glanced down at food on their plates, or upward at the ceiling vaults and the cumbersome chandeliers that swayed, gently, in the icy drafts. One humorist a few places down—I'm not sure who this man was—said, quietly but audibly, "What happened to Doug's face? He looks beat up."

"He's been drinking," replied a second, nearby voice. There was no time to find out who had spoken. Hiram, from his great chair at the head of the oak table, announced abruptly, "Let us say grace"—our cue to stop talking, close our eyes, and bow heads in prayer.

"Dear Father, bless this supper we are about to eat, and bless us. Let us not fight unnecessarily, but help us to behave like gentlemen. Look after our brothers who are unable to make it to the table because of injuries, and forgive us for injuring them. Help us to love all creatures, men and animals, the fish and the birds, and every green thing. Guard our red library against electrical fires in the walls, and keep out the rain, the cold, and trespassers. Please help us preserve our way of life. A special prayer from all of us for Doug, who has promised to stand in as quarterback this coming Sunday and throw the ball against the Episcopal Ministers. Amen."

"Amen. Amen," echoed voices all around. The official eating began. Water pitchers and peas in bowls traveled from hand to hand down the table. My plate was, unfortunately, still empty. Allan was sitting in my chair. I pushed my way toward the main course and prayed there would be some left. Of course there's never enough of anything. The wine carafes were already running empty. Wind shook the windowpanes and blew out the candles giving light to the table. Suddenly a large bat darted overhead—so close to our heads, in fact, you could hear its leathery wings as it veered away, barely missing things—and the young fathers ducked. At that moment quite a few cross-table shouting matches were under way:

"What?"

"That's *not* what he said!"

"Ask Anton. He's been depressed all his life. Hey, Anton, has it worked for you?"

"All I can say is when you're sick, you've got to take care of yourself!"

"What?"

"I heard him clearly because I was standing right beside him at the exact moment he fell!"

"Those poor people!"

"Who?"

"Anton's not here!"

"I can't hear!"

"He said, 'The God is *beyond* us'!"

"Has anyone seen the sheepdog?"

"That's not what he said!"

"I said he has a broken nose and a bad bump on his head and some shallow cuts on his hands and face!"

"Benedict, get your beetles away!"

"I have to tell you that that's not what he *said*! I was right there beside the man and you weren't even in the room at the time!"

"Who?"

"I believe it was his shoulder!"

"Depression is a serious illness!"

"Place your bets! Place your bets!"

"What?"

"*What?*"

All this shouting and noise soon reached a level at which

it was impossible to really *hear* anything. This can create a feeling of detachment, a comforting but utterly false sense of one's separateness from the busy crowd. It was in precisely this kind of isolated, subjective haze that I wandered around the table in search of red wine.

My plate was in my hand. I circled around back of Hiram's chair. Hiram wore his napkin as a bib tucked into his shirt collar. It was good to see him taking nourishment. His teeth were working and he appeared contented. I strolled on by. Brothers in a line were having their feed, and I said hello to each in turn. "Hello, Porter." "Hello, Eric." "Hello, Frank." "Hello, Jim." "Hello, Dennis." Someone had stacked paperbacks on the floor and I stumbled across these. I had to hold on to a chair to keep my balance—it was George's empty chair, and I would've sat in it but this was out of the question because taking George's chair would have been considered unforgivable, so I continued around the enormous table, behind the matching twins seated in a line. Sure enough, four or five beetles marched up the long table. Men in their seats cheered. Bob leaned over the table, put his head down behind a beetle, and blew—an illegal ploy to speed a lethargic insect. A beetle bumped into a glass and could go no farther. Another crawled into butter and this caused laughter. The beetle struggled helplessly in the butter—it was like some beetle tar pit—and a twin, seeing his opportunity, raised a plate to smash it. I couldn't watch. Cold casserole was left in the bottom of a ceramic bowl and I overturned this onto my plate. I did not have a fork so stood in place and ate with my fingers while watching the chandeliers overhead swing back and forth, back and forth on their ropes. It was the wind moving them. Twenty golden pendulums. This way and that they swung, not in unison but each according to its own particular frequency and gentle pitch and roll. Our chandeliers blown by wind became massive, crystal chimes. It was disturbing to watch these lights swinging so wildly, but on the other hand it was true that on account of bats our tall windows had been flung open, and this was the beginning, the first storm rolling through, the first snow in late autumn, winter's eve.

A triplet waving a tennis racket dashed after a black bat resting on a red wall. Tennis rackets are more effective against bats than nets, though also more grisly. I was one among several men gazing intently up toward the ceiling. I worried that a swinging chandelier might stress its rope, break free, and crash down on our heads. I could see, looking at the ceiling, the full extent of water damage up there. Fissures spread across vaults and from vault to vault; these black crevices intersected and formed, at their junctures, broad, open craters, pitted hollows bordered with plaster fragments that hung precariously, ready to fall and strike us. In the moving light from windblown chandeliers these vertical outcroppings cast shadows that swept metronomically across the broken, spackled vaults. Here and there moisture dripped. One great brown stain looked, I thought, exactly like a man's head. It was the profile of a man. Yes. Pointing north was his Celtic nose. There were the recessed eyes. Chipped paint made a gray mustache that concealed a familiar, weak mouth. There was even a cigarette formed by exposed timber, one of the sagging structural supports bearing the weight of ceiling, roof, snow. "Look at that," I said to my brothers gathered around.

"What?" asked one.

"Above the table. See?"

"Where?"

"There," pointing out, to Vincent, Bob, and Frank, the silhouette on the ceiling, the face blemished by scattered black holes. "I don't see a thing," Bob said; and Vincent, squinting to see past lights, asked, "Do you mean that cement about to drop in the salad?"

"To the left of that. One vault over. Watch the chandelier swing this way and you'll see it. Wait a minute. There it is. Notice the chin?" I continued to point and soon others joined in and peered up. Their heads tilted back and their eyes searched for the angry face that came and went with every changing shadow.

"I think I see. It's right up there! It's France," exclaimed our Bob.

"France?" I said.

"Sure. The hole in the middle is Paris, and that joint compound would be the English Channel."

"That is not the English Channel," I told Bob.

"It looks like a big wet spot to me!" Frank said, and laughed. Others laughed along, and Clay, true to form, blurted an off-color joke about prostate glands. Clearly none of these men could see what was right before their eyes. It's understandable, in a way, and typical among men in this family, men everywhere in our culture, I suppose, that they'll resort to hilarity in the face—no pun intended—of sorrow.

"They don't *want* to see the face on the ceiling, Doug," said a voice behind me. I turned to greet this person. It was Benedict. I was glad to see him. He looked me up and down. "What happened to your eye, Doug?"

"I got kicked."

"Who kicked you?"

"Hiram."

Benedict nodded at this. What more needed saying? Together we resumed looking up at the ceiling, its elaborate shadows, the clustered lights. "Uncanny resemblance, isn't it?" said Benedict.

"Yes."

"I remember when we were children and Father got mad at us for some inconsequential thing or other. Don't play in the rose garden! Don't steal your brothers' money! Quit beating up on Virgil! Father always looked exactly like that. Cigarette and all."

"You remember him well?"

"Not that well."

Benedict took a drink from his wineglass. He stuck his nose in the glass, inhaled deeply like the connoisseur he was. I watched him swirl what remained in the glass.

"But you remember things about him?"

"It's hard to say. We were so young then, and there were so many of us, practically all ages, you know, running all over creation."

I pressed him: "You must have had some interaction with the man. You were always a top student. You were head of the class, year after year. He must have been proud of *you*. You won all the prizes. You got *everything,* didn't you? You didn't have to worry about anything. It all went your way, didn't it? Doors opened for you. You were like some prince, practically. Shit."

At that moment a distant brother's high voice rose loudly above all others in the crowd. It was hard to say whom the voice belonged to. We ignored this shouting, and Benedict said, "Personal memories have questionable value, Doug."

This was something I couldn't agree with and I told him so, adding, "Our memories may not constitute exact and faithful historical records. However, they are, I think, fairly accurate indicators of perceptions and emotions. Our feelings tell us how things are with us! Wouldn't you agree with that? We each accumulate memories and insights and feelings, and these are ours to interpret and understand as we choose."

"You're right as usual. I can't argue with that," said Benedict.

"Of course it all gets to be a muddle after a while, particularly in families."

"Yes, it does."

"Everyone has his own private past."

"Hmn."

"A hundred different stories. A thousand different dinners."

"The math is discouraging." Benedict swirled his wine. The shouting at the dinner table had grown in volume. A fight had apparently broken out between hostile table companions wedged too closely together. It was unclear whether anyone had struck anyone yet. Probably—I'm basing this on past evenings and the absolute regularity with which some drunk hits another sitting a chair or two away—one brother had reached out and, in one of those routine moments of bitter frustration, smacked another. It was impossible to know for certain because of the gathered onlookers swarming, backs blocking the view. These backs were shoulder to shoulder, pressed tight, lined up and swaying gently as the spectators craned forward to get a better look. Noises escaped the crowd, and it was difficult to say which gasps came from the audience, which came from fighters. Someone cried out in what sounded like pain. The object of the violence was likely either food or a dredged-up childhood unhappiness. Contestants surrounded by voyeurs shouted vulgarly. I raised my own voice, hollered over the fight's sounds, "Think about it, Benedict! All of us with our private memories! People! Places! Feelings!"

"Yes, yes," Benedict agreed. "Tell me, Doug, what do *you* remember?"

"Me?"

I had to meditate on this. So many things came briefly to mind. Coconut cake. The taste of dirt. Asthma attacks.

Father's shoes and the sound at night of Virgil crying in his bed.

"Our rose garden in bloom," I said to Benedict, "and the games we played as children on warm summer afternoons. Remember the rose garden, Benedict? Those red and those dull pink blossoms? And the yellow grass in the meadow beyond the wall, the wildflowers blowing in the wind? Remember tree leaves whispering in the breeze? Do you remember, Benedict, how starlings flocked to our trees, how they suddenly, inexplicably, took flight? Whirling black tornadoes of birds. Birds by the thousand. Fantastic. Where have they gone? The starlings? It's all crows and homeless people now. What were our games? Do you remember our games? There was hide-and-seek, though it's true that there were never very many hiding places in the rose garden. We preferred blindman's bluff, because it gave us a chance to tie a scarf over Virgil's eyes and lead him with our calls into a thorny bush. We never got tired of that, did we? Virgil was so trusting. Sometimes we had a ball and then we played kill-the-man-with-the-ball. Do you remember kill-the-man-with-the-ball, Benedict? Someone was always getting ground into the dirt and crushed practically to death beneath a pile. We broke Irv's collarbone. He took it like a man. That was one of my favorite games. Or dodgeball! Remember dodgeball? You threw the ball as hard as you could at your opponents. What was the point of that game, anyway? Were there rules at all? Younger boys cried with fear when we played dodgeball. They could never run fast enough to get away. They didn't have the physical coordination to escape being hit. The object, I recall, was to run them down and slam the ball into their heads. Do you remember? Do you remember the games we played together in the rose garden? All those games! We were young! We didn't mean any harm! Not really. We were always sorry when someone got hurt. We were only playing. Do you remember, Benedict? Do you remember how the starlings took flight from the trees and everyone stopped playing and stared up into the sky above the meadow? That was when you could really slam the ball into someone's head. Do you remember our beautiful rose garden in bloom?"

Benedict seemed to think. His face had a troubled look. He seemed to be thinking quite hard. Finally he shook his head and said, "The rose garden? In bloom? Are you sure, Doug?"

"Well, things do get blurry with the passing years," I admitted to Benedict after a moment.

Benedict drank again from his wineglass. I said to him, "Where did you get that?"

"There was a carafe. It's probably empty by now."

"Damn."

"You can have some of mine if you want," Benedict said, offering his glass. "I don't like to drink too much red wine because it gives me a headache. It affects me in my work the next day."

"How is your work going?" I asked him as I accepted the glass with its mouthful of claret in the bottom. It was a small amount and I couldn't imagine that Benedict really wanted me to drink only *some* wine and pass the rest back. Or did he? If I finished Benedict's wine—and I had not been invited, expressly, to do this—it might be rude. On the other hand, there was no point in drinking only half, because this would not be enough. Should I finish Benedict's wine? Should I leave a polite amount? I stood still and gazed down into the glass and contemplated this problem. As a result I did not hear what Benedict was saying about his current experiments with beetles. So I wasn't certain, exactly, what he was referring to, when he announced, "In many respects, they're a lot more like us than we realize, Doug."

"Who are?"

"The invertebrates."

"Right. Yes. I see." Obviously Benedict referred to the crowd all leaning together, swaying left then right while watching the fight at the dinner table. The fight was breaking up. One brother was hauled to his feet while another, already standing, supported by many arms, walked slowly to a soft chair. A third lay motionless on the floor, and a nearby fourth—it was hard to be sure at such a distance but it looked like Henry or, more likely, Stephen—stood bent over at his waist, hands clutching his stomach in the archetypal posture of a man who has been kicked. I clutched Benedict's glass by its crystal stem. The wine looked good, too good not to polish off. My mouth tasted like clay and my jaw felt tight. My heart pounded quickly and irregularly, and my hands trembled. I lifted the glass to my mouth. The glass shook in my hand. I drank without spilling; the wine was dry, and its bouquet lingered in the glass. I held the liquid in my mouth, letting it soothe my mouth. Then I swallowed and the wine became a warming stream that trickled down my throat. This warmth spread outward, into my chest—it felt like a warm little bomb splashing in my heart, sending shock waves through the blood. Right away my heart's pounding diminished. The muscles in my jaw relaxed. My shivering hands fell still again, as I said:

"Ah."

Remembering starlings and games, I peered up at our broken ceiling. There was the face. It seemed to watch over me and my brother sharing a glass. Smoke from other brothers' between-course cigarettes ascended in white clouds around the face; the smoke blew this way and that in the wind, and it looked as if this smoke had billowed out from the face's mouth and from the blunt end of that cigarette-like ceiling beam that ran between vaults.

The face, smoking, became lifelike. Changing shadows cast by moving lights animated it, gave it expressiveness—the face appeared to scowl, then grin. It appeared to open its mouth, as if preparing to speak. Seeing this, I listened hard.

I heard the Doberman's teeth gnawing bone. I heard the wind rushing in, blowing more manuscript papers from a writing desk. I heard the soprano singing and close to a hundred men's bass, baritone, and tenor voices talking and arguing. I heard cutlery, our forks and knives scraping plates; and

I heard chair legs scuff the floor as someone pushed back his chair to stand and stumble off to the bathroom. I heard cursing.

Listening harder, I heard water dripping, minuscule drops falling from the ceiling, splashing our books in the unlit stacks. I heard the twenty golden ropes, creaking under their burdens of chandeliers. I heard Donovan urging Hiram to "Take your time and chew your food," and I heard a triplet's tennis racket smash a flying black bat.

That's a sickening noise.

The dripping water splashed. My neck felt sore from looking up. I did not want to turn away from the speaking mouth. A light fixture swung and its bulbs flickered, and in this instant the mouth on the ceiling opened wide and smoke appeared to pour out, a vast, poisonous exhalation. Someone had lit a joint! That familiar dope aroma smelled delicious. The fact is, I'll take a puff of marijuana late in the evening.

The mouth opened, more smoke poured out, and a voice I had not heard since childhood said:

*"Stop drinking so much! You'll destroy yourself and everyone you care for! Do you want to end up a drunk? Do you want to die a drunk?"*

"What?" I said.

But the face had vanished. I had to wait a moment for the lights to swing back into correct position, for shadows to line up again, for the smoking mouth to continue talking.

"What do you want from me, Dad?" I asked the ceiling. Everywhere, my brothers ranged around. I noticed several serious fellows staring at me, watching me watch for the return of the wrathful face. "Come back! Tell me what to do!" I called into the air as, one more time, at their great height, our twenty chandeliers swung along their arcs and the long shadows swept across the ceiling. The lights aligned, and the great brown water stain, so far away, became, once more, the face.

My hands had begun shaking again. I could feel, deep in my neck, the beginnings of a tension headache. The syringes in my coat pocket were pressed hard against my chest. Everything was moving and spinning. Our fire blazed in our fireplace. Sounds echoed wildly. I heard the sinister grinding made by the Doberman's teeth chewing that bone. I heard whispers from my brothers nearby. Snowflakes blew in through open windows and I felt like laughing. There was an acrid smell of wine; a few violet drops remained pooled in the glass in my hand. Drink it? Give it back? Drink it? Give it back? Whom was I kidding? The mouth on high opened to say its words. I was sure I could almost, almost, hear those words. "Father has something to say!" I shouted at my brothers. The soprano sang German, the dog barked; and the smell of marijuana grew stronger and stronger in the room. "Pass that joint, brother," I cried loudly to nobody in particular. Then I hoisted the glass and drank the wine. I hadn't even gotten a pork chop, and that dog had eaten a big one. Nevertheless, I was laughing.

How good it felt to laugh. The laughter came in magnificent waves. It wasn't as if anything seemed particularly funny. Where, for instance, was my plate? I must've set it on an empty chair. This made me laugh. Small accidents were happening everywhere I looked. Brothers hurt in falls or fights were piling up on sofas and recliners, and our room had begun to resemble one of those wartime hospitals set up in a crumbling manor house. Someone on a chaise moaned, another voice called for water, and Samaritans made rounds, puffing up cushions and administering cordials. This always happens around midnight. Pretending injury is a good way to get a drink in this house.

"Oh! My foot! My foot!" I cried. No one seemed to hear. I hopped up and down to create the impression of a muscle cramp or sprain. I bent over, reached down, and made a show of massaging the calf of my left leg. I peeked up to see if anyone had noticed. I stood, wobbled lamely, shook out the "bad" leg, and made a terrible grimace, a face showing pain. None of this drew any attention. I hobbled a few steps and leaned heavily on a chair back, said to the nearest man, "Lester? Can you help me?"

"What's up, Doug?"

"My foot." I made a face. Lester stared back at me, at my black eye and bloody shirtfront, at my rug-burned hand and arm. I explained to him, "I was hurrying to get a pork chop and I fell."

"That's too bad, Doug. Here, sit down. Let me give you a

hand. There's nothing worse than a carpet burn. You should put vitamin E on that. Wow, that's one nice purple shiner around that eye. I guess you won't be playing against the Episcopal Ministers this Sunday."

This had not occurred to me. How convenient. "Probably not. The ankle feels like it's swelling."

"Roll down your sock and let's take a look. Hmn. It doesn't appear to be swollen. Does this hurt?"

"Ow!" I said, convincingly I hoped. Lester pressed the ankle at several points, and each time I exclaimed dramatically, "Easy!" or "Don't!" or "Hurts!"

"You should apply ice to that," he advised. "You want to elevate it, too, for drainage. I'm personally not in favor of bandaging. I believe the joint heals more strongly if it's allowed to rotate."

"I agree." My chair was comfortable. I rested my foot on an ottoman. Electric light reflected dimly off windowpanes; as our chandeliers swayed in the wind, light played and the glass seemed to sparkle and glow. The fact that the windows were exceedingly dirty no doubt had something to do with this pleasing, nighttime effect. Snow blew in and shallow puddles dripped from the sills. A few bats flew loops around the chandelier ropes. I looked up for the smoking face, but it was no longer present. Certainly Father would reappear, eventually, and I would see him and hear him speak. It was getting late, but there was, I felt, plenty of time for everything. I was happy to be sitting, and I hoped Lester would volunteer to fetch ice for my foot. I have always felt that Lester is one of the nicest and most compassionate of all people. I said to him, "Ice would be just the thing."

"Why don't you stay here and relax and I'll bring some from the bar, Doug."

"Would you, Lester? You're kind," I said, working my way to the real point. "Lester, I hate to be a bother, but if you're going to the bar—since you're going anyway?—I wonder if you might bring back a short whiskey? Straight up? While you're at it?"

"It's unwise to drink when you're injured, Doug. Alcohol is an anesthetic. You don't want to dull this pain too much, because you're going to be moving around on that ankle and you'll want to feel what hurts and what doesn't. That way you won't wreck it permanently."

What nonsense. I felt like shouting at him. What was the man *thinking*? I wasn't a child! I was an adult and could fend for myself.

I whimpered, "Just a taste, Lester. Please?"

"Well."

"Please?"

He went, then. Thank God. Lester is friendly to a fault and this makes him a pest. It wasn't as if I were literally *suffering*. So many among us were. I heaved in a deep breath and relaxed in my overstuffed armchair, surveyed the room strewn with the fallen, waited for whiskey. In certain respects I was, I suppose, suffering. My arm hurt and my head where Hiram had kicked it was throbbing; the eye was closing up; if Lester made it back, I could use the ice on the hematoma. This wasn't the first time I'd been kicked in the head by one of my brothers. Once, in a fit of sadness and longing, I had dropped to the floor and nuzzled a pair of brand-new steel-toed work boots. Those hurt.

Temperatures were plummeting in the red library. The fire in our fireplace burned brightly but without effect. I shivered. Water splashed from the ceiling's leaks. Snow amassed in drifts on the windowsills. It was a blizzard. I gathered my sport coat snugly around me. The coat's pockets were spilling over, spilling over with the used hypodermic needles, the stoppered vials, and Barry's stethoscope. Having these objects, I felt prepared for the balance of our evening, come what may. It happened that several books rested on a three-legged table beside my chair. Imagine my delight at discovering among these volumes our long-lost—misshelved, presumably—copy of A. C. Fox-Davies's oversize *A Complete Guide to Heraldry,* a work notable not only for its splendid illuminated crests going back to the twelfth century, but for the rare zeal of this author's loving exegesis of the modern quest to establish family and rank in a world so often indifferent to lineage. Here was a book I'd loved as a boy. Unfortunately, exposure to moisture had bloated and fused its pages, and try as I might, I was unable to tug apart its leather covers or open it to a clean page. Someone must have left *A Complete Guide to Heraldry* beneath a drip or beside an unclosed window. How could anyone treat a work of this beauty and importance with such disregard? What

I am trying to say is that even though this is a *library*—a better-than-average private library holding diverse collections (our Restoration Poems and Plays, our Patriotic Songs, etc.), all worth, probably, loads of money, that is if they were properly cataloged instead of casually abandoned in piles with sweating cocktail glasses leaving rings—as I was saying, even though the red library is a first-rate private repository, our books are invariably taken down and handled with carelessness approaching contempt. It is difficult for me not to abhor my beloved brothers whenever I come across their examples of common destructiveness. On these occasions when the sight of waterlogged novels, cigarette-branded tables, coffee-stained pillow shams, and frayed draperies puts me in mind of death, I like nothing better than a solitary stroll through the dark and dusty stacks.

How the time passes in those enchanted corridors filled with forgotten treasures.

But tonight as on all nights following dinner the stacks were inhabited by certain men who, having excused themselves and left the table, retire, for a while, from company and disappear into the library's unlit districts. There, hidden by shadows, they lean against shelves or walk from aisle to aisle. If you look hard, you can see them aimlessly, furtively skulking, their hands sunk deeply into pockets, eyes peering down at the floor until one fellow brushes past another and each looks up briefly. This is an odd business, and slightly menacing, my brothers' surreptitious, intrafamilial, homosexual cruising. It's not that I disapprove, entirely. But why do it *here,* in a domestic setting? Reclining in my tattered armchair, I could hear boots' soles scuffing the floorboards. I could hear, from deep in the stacks, murmurs and quiet, hushed coughs.

Clearly it was later in the evening than I had thought. Even Gunner the Doberman seemed edgy. Over to my chair he came with his gnawed bone.

"Hello, boy."

Gunner stared at me with his dog's eyes. Up close, he seemed gigantic. His coat shimmered and he had little or no fat on his body. That bone hung in his mouth.

"Sit?" I said.

Gunner's teeth glistened. Instead of sitting he came closer. He stood beside my chair. He stuck his nose over one chair arm, as if he were maybe thinking of dropping the porkchop bone in my lap. But that wasn't what he was thinking. He kept possession of his bone. It was pitted and scarred from his teeth.

"There's a nice dog." I slowly, hesitantly raised my hand to pet Gunner's head. He growled through wet incisors clenched around the bone. Quickly I removed my hand. Gunner stared hungrily at my shirtfront, and I imagined he scented Maxwell's blood there. I could smell the dog's horrible breath. Fear of animals is atavistic, and humans presume that animals perceive this fear. I presumed this about Gunner. There was no one nearby who could rescue me; I was alone in my chair; I had nothing with which to shield myself except A. C. Fox-Davies's *A Complete Guide to Heraldry.*

There we sat, dog and man. I imagined this Doberman as a kind of animal fiend, instinctually drawn to my blood-smeared shirt. I pictured Gunner releasing the pork bone, then leaping powerfully forward, attacking the shirt, driving sopping teeth through cotton cloth into my chest, puncturing my lungs or my heart. I barely breathed. Facing the dog, my sad copy of *A Complete Guide to Heraldry* clenched in my hands, I felt deliciously close to death.

Elsewhere people came and went, played card games and chess, tended to one another's injuries, chased the bats. These men's lives seemed, for the moment, untouched by fear. But I did not envy them. I felt the way humans must have felt in earlier times, at the dawn of our history, when the world was alive with primitive dangers and life depended for its preservation on the graces and fancies of hateful gods.

"Go ahead, kill me," I commanded the dog. He held on to his bone. What was he thinking? There was no way of knowing. He was just a dog.

Winds blew and the music played. Snow piled up. People talked but I was not paying attention to their conversations. I felt the cold air. Gunner's eyes shimmered and I held my book close to me. It was easy, looking into the dog's mouth, at those white teeth and black gums, to imagine the power and authority our ancestors must have felt with companions like Gunner at their sides.

What an animal. What was he doing with an alcoholic like Chuck for a master?

"You understand about death, don't you?" I said to him.

He growled quietly then readjusted the bone, expertly, in his teeth. Snap snap. I regarded this as an answer of sorts. I confided to the Doberman, "Once upon a time men celebrated the seasons of death and rebirth with sacrifices and burnt offerings. The world was cold and forbidding, and if you didn't watch out, your enemies would come up behind you and kill you with a spear or a club. A single night's foul weather could destroy your crops, and then you might starve. Each day brought terror. Angry spirits unleashed thunder and lightning, diseases and pestilences, every species of ferocious beast. Men developed language to communicate their terror to one another. People were in pain all the time. They believed they would be rewarded for their pain. This is what is known as the human condition."

It seemed to me that the dog was paying attention. What a fierce nose Gunner had. Perhaps he knew, from my serious tone of voice, that I was speaking on weighty matters. I told him, "Over the years mankind has devised many ways to alleviate the pain of living, and much of human history can be understood as a death march toward this goal. Although suffering in life can sometimes be postponed, it can never be avoided. This is the central lesson of the world's religions. Please don't drool on the book. All right, Gunner? Good boy. This is the central lesson of the world's religions. Where was I? The pain of existence is ours to bear. In order to bear it we must make sacrifices. We must offer ourselves up before God and our fellow man. That is the function of the Corn King."

The dog really did appear to be listening. It was as if he knew—was letting me know that he knew—what I was talking about. Of course I realize it would be going too far to suggest that animals comprehend the symbolic realm. But I gave Gunner the benefit of the doubt. "The Corn King is an archetypal harvest spirit. His story is as old as recorded time. In rude societies, before the dawn of civilization, when it was believed that spirits resided in all things, in the mountains and lakes, trees and grasses, cats and dogs"—I gave Gunner a smile; his ears pricked up and I went on—"no spirit was regarded with greater awe than the spirit of the corn. From corn came food and grain alcohol. Life depended on the harvest, and so human beings were routinely sacrificed to ensure the fertility of the crop. These were martyrs. While alive—and death was painful, very painful, Gunner—the Corn King's human representatives were worshiped as gods. It was their blood that enriched the earth, their tears that brought the rains, their flesh that fatted the land. They died so that others might live. Today, mimicry of this ancient practice is common in many popular religions." At this point the dog began to lose interest. He made a yawning sound and fiddled with the bone in his mouth. I quickly said, "In some instances, the Corn King's still-beating heart was cut out and devoured!"

I felt nervous telling Gunner this. That blood on my shirtfront was a perfect target. We've all heard the frightening stories of domesticated animals regressing into feral states and tearing their owners limb from limb. Gunner had made short work of that pork chop. The dog's nose twitched. Perhaps he had eaten enough. I explained to him that modern men had lost touch with ancient rhythms of death and regeneration, but that it was possible—if you took intoxicants and wore the right mask and costume—to regain connection with the primeval aspects of the Self, and to enact, in ritualized form, the important celebrations of sacrifice and abasement; that this was, in some respects, what family get-togethers were all about. I wrapped up, "You see, Gunner, the Corn King is my gift to my brothers. Every year I have a few drinks, then get in costume, and they try to catch me. Luckily, most of those guys are out of shape. Ultimately, the Corn King must die. In this way the family of man can prosper and thrive."

This ended my talk with the dog. But Gunner did not back off right away. First he allowed me to pet his head. What a pleasant creature. He only wanted what we all want from time to time, to submit and feel love. "Gunner, how would you like to be my dog?"

My fear of him was gone. In fear's place was a new self-possession; I understood why people keep animals. I rose from my chair—carefully holding *A Complete Guide to Heraldry* in front of my body, just to be safe—and I didn't even bother pretending to have a hurt foot. So what if Lester said something? It was late and the time had come at last to go over to the African masks, choose a colorful headdress from the wall, put it on my head, then run around and shout the kinds of obscenities that get people mad.

"Come on, Gunner."

Together this dog and I padded quietly past the injured sprawled on the sofas, past the men lying on pillows or simply facedown on our colorful rug. Along the way I peered up to see whether Father's face had reappeared while I was getting acquainted with Gunner. But there was no face, only the brown water stain, made darker by a new leak running from the area where Father's mouth would be, if Father were present. A bunch of men were convened around the big leather sofa. They called to me as I approached, "Doug! Think fast!"

I looked up and saw a sofa pillow flying through the air at me. The pillow was blue and I wouldn't've seen it had it not worn gold, braided tassels. These caught the light and I caught the pillow, and Seamus, our coach, hollered, "Good reflexes, Doug. Bring that pillow in."

There was nothing to do except cooperate. Seamus said, "Doug, you're a veteran quarterback so I'm going to let you call your own plays." Then Angus kindly pointed out the scrimmage line—it was the place where our Bokhara's rich blue border meets red—and I placed the pillow right on this woven border, and Seamus said, "The rug is the field."

We huddled. Gunner stuck his wet nose into the huddle. That made eight of us plus the Doberman, who could be counted on to growl at oncoming rushers. I got down on one knee, peered up into my brothers' faces.

We were not young men. Not at all. None of us wore the right kind of shoes. I said, "What in Gods name are we doing this for at this hour?"

"What time is it?" asked Nick.

"It's after two," Ralph said, and Angus asked, "Can it be that late?" and Gregory said, "I don't see how," but Frank insisted, "It is after two," and Angus argued, "But we just ate," to which Ralph replied, "We ate hours ago." I interrupted, "Quiet in the huddle. Pay attention. Has anyone got anything to drink? The quarterback needs a drink."

After that our huddle did fall quiet. You could feel, I thought, that everyone was a little depressed.

I told the team, "I'll fake a handoff to Angus. Angus, go short up the weak side and cut left at the third reindeer. Nick, go wide down the line along Intellectual History. Topper, go for the long toss up the middle over Maxwell, then fake like you're going to high-step over Virgil, but cut across Barry instead."

We lined up. Facing us on defense were drunks. The dog, my constant companion, trotted up and—when Mongo bent over to hike the tasseled blue pillow—sniffed between Mongo's legs. I tugged Gunner out of the way, stuck my hands where the dog's face had been—it felt warm between Mongo's legs—and called:

"Hike."

It's hard to say what happened after that. Mongo shoved the pillow into my hands and I faked the handoff to Angus. Angus ran off and vanished directly into Eighteenth Century Novels while Topper bolted down the rug. Nick fell down and Gregory crunched Bob, and you could hear an audible crack like vertebrae snapping when Bob collapsed in a heap. I noticed Lester standing by the sidelines with an ice chunk in one hand and my whiskey in the other, so I zigzagged over and exclaimed, "Lester, the ankle got better by itself! Isn't that remarkable? I won't be needing the ice! Thanks anyway." I ran in place while Mongo blocked for me and Lester held out the whiskey. I grabbed this from Lester, drank, then handed back the empty glass and returned to the game refreshed. Right away I could see that there were too many things happening at once. Nick had picked himself up and made a beeline down the stacks, then gotten involved in an argument with several twins. Topper had made good progress down the carpet and was darting back and forth, back and forth, leaping over Virgil, leaping over Barry, trying to get in the open. Frank and Joe butted heads and Frank toppled backward. Gunner sniffed Bob. Topper plowed into a coffee table and there was a disturbing crash. The chandeliers blinked; visibility was a problem. I was standing beneath the water stain, and I looked up at this, and suddenly—just as I was getting positioned to lob the pillow to Topper standing tall on the broken table, excitedly waving his arms—suddenly there was Father, up in the lights, looking incredibly huge and damp on our decomposing ceiling, puffing his cigarette and staring straight down at me.

Father's mouth opened. Leaking black water poured from the ceiling as he commanded:

"*Run.*"

I tucked that pillow under my arm, stepped left to avoid being tackled by Clay, spun to the right for no reason at all, and tore off down the carpet. Far in the distance were the African masks, and I suppose I was aiming to race down and snag one off the wall, put it on, and wear it as a helmet. From every side, men charged after me. "Kill the man with the ball!" a voice shouted, and I knew that I was doomed. I could hear—and feel, through our rotting floorboards—my brothers' dozens of thundering, running, stomping shoes. It seemed to me as I fled my brothers that it would be good if we could, at some point, get together, stop trying to kill each other, and find Father's ashes—take care of that urn, so that these inconvenient, late-night visitations might not take place, and people would not have to get hurt.

The shoes stampeded toward me down the antique carpet. Gales forced snow through our open windows. I dashed between two chairs, then veered off course to avoid a triplet. Gunner was right behind me and he cornered violently and I heard his claws tearing the rug. We were running away from the African masks. My eye was swollen and I could not see well. "Lead the way, Gunner," I called to the Doberman, and sure enough the dog sprinted out ahead of me and bounded over a low table that seemed to rise out of nowhere. I jumped with all my might and sailed over and landed on the icy floor without breaking a single ashtray, vase, or empty glass. This gave me hope and made me feel that I was not an old man. Youthful feelings did not last because I can never allow myself to feel good for very long. The dog skittered through slushy ice piled high beneath the windows. I glanced out a window and was relieved to see that the bad weather had reduced visibility, and that the fires in our meadow were little more than faraway lights, glowing, almost fading, set beautifully against the night.

Out of sight, out of mind, as they say.

And already I was having trouble breathing. I clutched the sofa pillow. Men pursuing me were not far behind. The Doberman regarded me with mournful eyes. I whispered to him, "Everything is going to be all right, Gunner."

"Kill Doug! Kill the Corn King! Carve out his heart!" a voice called. I turned and watched Clay vault over the coffee table. Behind Clay came Gregory. After Gregory came Arthur, Rex, Pierce, Kevin, Vaughan, and—at the rear of this line, though not far behind and moving forward quickly, taking long strides and towering over other men—Zachary. Another group of ten approached from the north, cutting off escape in this direction. Stragglers grabbed knives from our dinner table and made serpentine runs around card tables and chairs. "Go this way! Go that way!" men yelled. Windows rattled and the rotting curtains sailed upward on drafts of air. Siegfried, Porter, Raymond, and Tom jogged in a group across the rug. Siegfried was sweating and red in the face beneath lights that dangled like clock weights over all our heads; and the water streamed down in a river from Father's mouth; and somewhere in the near distance another article of glass or china crashed to the floor. I said, "Gunner, we

need to hide," and the dog wagged his tail then dashed immediately off through the snow and ice.

The dog led me into a shadowy region between rows of
shelves that held boxes. The boxes were unmarked, identical,
gray, taped shut. Water dripped loudly around us, and some
was collected in pools on the uneven floor. We splashed
through. Gunner sniffed at boxes stacked on the lower
shelves. His nose led him down the aisle of boxes. Together
we stalked along. The narrow and damp passageway became
darker and darker, and it seemed—though of course this
could not have been the case; there were no stairs here—that
the dog and I were descending into another realm of the library, going down through some old, forgotten tunnel that
took us below and away from the lively center of things. In
fact, no place in the red library is terribly distant from any
other. Nor are there tunnels. This was a sensory illusion and
it meant that I was about to undergo a panic attack. The
noises of running men came from all around, a crashing riot
that caused the dog to whimper and me to sweat. I could feel
the floor vibrate as my brothers' feet sped by on the other
side of the boxes. From behind us and from up ahead came
mysterious, threatening sounds, little scuffs and bumps—as
if men were sneaking up to bushwhack us, or searching out
dark alcoves, hidden places for a person to lean back, stand
very still, and wait before jumping out. I was sure I could
hear breathing. This may have been water, dripping. Dust
covered dry stretches of floor and I saw that the dog and I
were leaving paw- and footprints, a wet trail. I knelt and

used the blue pillow to sweep the floor and erase tracks. The dust floated up. Ours were not the only prints visible on the floor. Someone wearing large shoes, size twelve or, possibly, thirteen, had passed this way. Falling water got louder as we walked along; and the air felt still and close; and the whole tunnel sensation grew acute. I felt entombed. Shelf after shelf of unlabeled boxes walled our passageway; and of course Gunner halted, from time to time, to sniff one. I whispered to him, "Gunner, we don't have time for that now," and remarkably, this dog seemed to understand. He abandoned the boxes and trotted ahead, claws clicking against the floor. Could the claws be heard at a distance? It did appear, from the economy and gentleness of the dog's movements, that, in spite of claws, Gunner was trying his best to avoid making noise. Brothers hunting in packs yelled to one another, and I was glad under the circumstances to have an animal helper. I whispered, "Go find the African masks," and Gunner stared at me blankly.

"Masks," I explained to the dog. It was unreasonable to expect him to comprehend, but we had been working so well together, and I had, I admit, gotten my hopes up. I raised my hands and mimed putting on a mask. I did a little dance, a few brisk steps in the water. I made faces— stretching my lips apart with my fingers, sticking my tongue out at the dog, trying to communicate—and pointed in the general direction, I thought, of the masks. Dogs don't understand pointing. I scolded, "Wooden masks! African masks! That way! On the wall by the door to the rare-book room! Next to the tiger! Quit licking your nuts and fetch me a mask!"

For good measure I gave him a kick in the butt. "Hurry, boy," I called as he disappeared down an aisle.

In my impatience with the dog I had forgotten, almost forgotten, for a moment, how scared I was.

Then William stepped out of nowhere and, in his hushed, baritone voice, said, "How dare you abuse Chuck's animal."

"William. God. You scared me." Panic was coming on and I was thirsty for a double whiskey and it did not help to be talking to a person who hides in the stacks acting like a wraith. I said to this impertinent man, "What are you talking about?"

"You were beating him."

"I was not. I gave him a friendly shove. It's called encouragement. You have to be firm with animals or they won't respect you."

"You sound like Father."

I was not certain how to respond to this. On the one hand, I felt complimented. On the other, I felt insulted. William said, "You think you know how people should behave. But you're the one who doesn't know how to behave, Doug. You mistreat people and you mistreat animals. You even mistreat flowers."

William's voice was barely audible, and in the dim light I could distinguish the outline of his face, though not

William's mouth or nose or eyes. He was dressed all in black, and his body in the dark seemed indistinct, borderless, a soft, porous form that lingered sickeningly before the shelves.

"I'm sorry about your lilies, William, but that was hours ago. It's not polite to hold grudges."

"Please don't tell me how to feel."

"I wasn't."

William confessed, "I used to like you but I'm not sure if I do anymore, Doug. I think there's something wrong with you. You think you're so important. You think we should all get down on our knees and pray to you. But you're not important. I hope they catch you tonight. I hope they catch the Corn King. I really do."

"Just tell me how to get out of here."

"Go that way."

Which way? Back the way I'd come? The dog had gone ahead. I did not want to lose the dog. I could see, looking farther down the tunnel, two or three smaller aisles branching from the main walkway. William said, "Take your first right through Minor Elizabethan Drama. Comedies will appear on your left and tragedies will be on your right. Keep going past *Ralph Roister Doister* and *The Spanish Tragedy*. About three shelves after *Gorboduc,* you'll come to a narrow fork. Do not continue through Shakespeare because that whole section is flooded and you'll ruin your shoes. Instead, you'll want to detour through Cavalier Poets and Writers of the Couplet. Go straight all the way to Hobbes. Follow Hobbes through The Age of Dryden, then veer left. This brings you face-to-face with Pope and Swift. You will not have noticed anything in translation. If you do encounter any French political writing, you'll know you're in the wrong corridor. You'll have to make a half-turn and backtrack through Sir Walter Scott. This is tricky. Be careful not to go too far because the Waverley novels will return you, inevitably, to *The Castle of Perseverance,* and you'll never get out. It's better to remain in the nineteenth century if you can get there. As you know, we've had shelving problems, so don't panic if you see Russians mixed in with the triple deckers. Put your head down and charge through the War Poets. By now you're smack in the center of The Modern Era. From here you can choose any number of directions. Pay attention because if you take the wrong route, you'll wind up running around in circles and you'll have to start over from *Beowulf.* Are you paying attention?"

"Yes."

"The New Critics. Stay with The New Critics and you'll get where you're going."

"Thank you."

"You're welcome."

Minor Elizabethans were not hard to find. These decrepit volumes were crammed onto shelves that sagged beneath the weight of crumbling bindings. Dust from the leather covers smelled oddly sweet; it was not unlike the smell of a very old person, a corporeal sweetness of glue and rotting paper and fading pigments. I was reminded of Hiram and promised myself I'd give the man a piece of my mind about friendship, kindness, and ordinary reciprocity in relationships. I could hear my brothers rampaging in the distance. And there were other ominous noises, things crashing and thudding. What in the world was happening in our red library? I forged ahead and soon, as William had promised, arrived at oily black water covering uneven floor beneath Shakespeare. "Gunner, what's taking you so long?" I whispered as I squeezed past neglected poets. It was tight in these aisles and I was afraid I'd get stuck. You could insert yourself into a cramped corner and get hopelessly trapped, and no one would hear your calls for help, and you could waste away and die while your brothers drank and broke furniture, or so I thought in my terror of the darkness and the solitude. How long had it been since anyone had come this way and taken down one of these privately printed old chestnuts with the pages that had probably, for all anyone knew, never been cut? Years? Decades? It seemed to me, as I shouldered my way through, that no one had *ever* been in this place—or ever would be again, once I had found my way out to the open spaces where a person could think and breathe clean air that was not contaminated with such horrible smells, the kinds of smells that make you want to run away, were it not so dark that running would be dangerous.

How odd, then, that someone was, in fact, running. Toward me. I could hear the footsteps and they were coming fast and getting louder, louder. I longed to have the Doberman with me. Where was that animal—oh, if only Gunner were *my* dog!—when I needed him? I had nothing but the blue pillow and Barry's stethoscope and those disposable hypodermic syringes crowded among the medicine vials in my jacket pocket. It was imaginable, to me, alone in our awful stacks—consider, if you will, my desperate, exhausted, late-night state of mind—that if attacked, I could hold the pillow before me as a soft-sculpture shield, while waving, threateningly, a syringe. This made a ridiculous picture, but on the whole it seemed better to wave a needle than to do nothing. I put my hand in my pocket and, carefully, fished out a syringe. Getting a good grip on it was a problem because I was holding the pillow and shaking all over from fear. The runner splashed through water and I pressed myself against a bookcase and stuck out my foot, and his foot hit mine and he exhaled a sound like "Ah" as he tumbled forward in the darkness. I could not make out who the man was, but suspected it was probably Angus, who had gone out for a short pass during football practice and disappeared into Eighteenth-Century Novels. I did hear, at the finish of the man's long, arcing fall, his body's collision with a shelf. The closest I can come to describing this sound is to say that it was the crunch a head of crispy lettuce might make if squashed beneath a steel tray. The fallen man groaned in pain, and I said to him, "Don't follow me or I'll stick you! Beware of the Corn King! Ha ha!" then quickly retreated in search of the main aisle. I was, as far as I could tell, lost in a maze of Liberal Theologians, Antiquaries, and Bibliographers; and water streamed across the floor; and my shoes were sodden; and all the excitement was having an effect on my bladder. It is true, absolutely, that a desire to urinate is intensified by any feeling of water against the skin. Throughout much of the eighteenth century, European gentlemen enjoyed the privilege of relieving themselves in the public squares. I unzipped and tugged it out. There is nothing quite like the primitive ecstasy of pissing somewhere besides the bathroom. I rate the act very highly. Pissing in nature or in some dark corner, as I was, captures and brings into consciousness certain archaic versions of a man's most secret Self—those aspects of character and identity that remain, in civilized daily life, veiled, disguised, sealed away: the messy, narcissistic, bodily Self of infancy; the wild, magnificent, feral Self of mankind's prehistoric beginnings; that communal, loving Self expressed in each man's deep bond with his fellow men; and of course the sovereign, assertive, fiercely territorial Self that announces, Get out of my way! I'm taking a leak!

Feeling such emotions, it was impossible not to elevate the stream and hose down, as they say, a few literary masterpieces.

I may as well point out that I was able to hit titles all the way up on the third and fourth shelves. When you get into your middle years, as I have, these things matter.

I shook and put it away. Since I'm being frank, I ought to say that I went through the mature man's generic *process* of shaking: several rapid shakes followed by a brief rest followed by more jiggling, and the whole ordeal repeated until everything feels comfortably dry and secure. As I grow longer in the tooth, I find myself shaking off for greater and greater stretches of time, and I always use this time to fret morosely about my health in general, and about the likelihood that a grave illness, conceivably located in the bladder region, will overtake me in the future, maybe imminently. In this way a pleasurable, natural act becomes the catalyst for somber reflections and an unnatural, incipient depression. So much of life follows this pattern exactly, I think. We begin to lose ourselves in a joyful or gratifying act—it can be a creature comfort or something complicatedly emotional like stimulating conversation or the solitary immersion in a poem, a beautiful landscape, or a work of art—and we forget, in the moment of serenity, all the pain and trouble of life. Until, quite suddenly and, as a rule, shockingly, this very forgetfulness, our fleeting holiday from care, becomes nothing more than another occasion to remember how truly infrequently happiness comes to us, and how likely we are to die in some horrible way. Then, disgusted with ourselves over our inability to enjoy life, we halt the pleasurable activity and move on, as speedily as we can, to other business. It was precisely this kind of dispirited self-loathing that led me to give myself only a few cursory shakes, so that when I replaced myself in my trousers, I felt urine dribbling down my leg. As always when this happens, I became enraged. I became angry and irrational. The night was cold, and I struggled against despair.

The struggle, however, was unavailing.

I wept.

At first I wept for myself—for my incontinence, obviously—and then for my entire, ridiculous existence, and for the loneliness I felt, not only there in the literature section in the late hours on that snowy night, but all the time, constantly, ever since I could remember feeling anything at all. As I wept, I felt lonelier and lonelier and lonelier. I envisioned, one after another, my brothers, the bloated, red faces of my brothers, all my beloved brothers but in particular Hiram and Virgil and Maxwell. These three I loved best. And also George. Would we ever see George again? After a while I was weeping for the rose garden and the former grandeur of our trees and lawns, those green fields where we played as children. We had always hurt one another in our games; hurting was the object of our games; and this made me cry more, and I held the blue pillow to my breast. I wrapped my arms around the blue pillow, hugged it to me, and let the tears come. I was standing in water up to my ankles, and this for some reason became another pressing sadness. I suppose it was because the water was rising that I felt so affected. Before long I was crying for, it seemed, everything. Everything in the red library was deserving of tears. Those eyeless, emaciated, deaf and dead animals on their barren squares of wall always reminded me of past Dougs, the Dougs who perished as youths; and, as I wept, they reminded me, the animals, of myself and of what would surely become of me one day, maybe soon. I was nothing but another Doug. Hiram was the oldest. Father I know, really, only from his occasional, shadowy appearances above the lights, his intermittent manifestations as a damp stain. Actually, this is not, strictly speaking, the whole truth. It is true in the sense that it describes the way I have felt for as long as I have known my feelings. I remember, I think, our father's face and his voice. I remember his mustache. I remember our father in his underwear at night. I remember the hair on his legs. I remember the smell in the bathroom after he left it. I remember his unhappiness and his dread of our happiness, and I remember him saying, "How's my Doug?" I remember his body's smells, his smells of tobacco, of course, and of alcohol and cologne, a cologne like lavender you never smell anymore. I remember the pleasure of seeing him enter the room. I remember certain stories and jokes. Actually, I forget the stories and the jokes, though I remember that these existed. I remember his conviction that he was hated, and I remember the thunder his footsteps made crossing the floor. Time after time my brothers and I have joined together to eat, drink, and bury that man. All we ever did was eat, drink, and injure each other. The sadness of our cruelty was more than I could bear. Tears rose in waves that washed up from the center of my body. The muscles in my sides felt as if they would tear from the strain of that sobbing. The water around my feet was steadily rising. I knew it was prideful to overinterpret broken pipes and a leaking roof, but on the other hand it did seem that I was not completely alone in my crying, that the red library was dripping and pouring out its own tears, its own remorse.

I thought these things because I had failed to shake off after urinating. What a degenerate I was. What sadness, to come to such a point in life, this point at which the simplest acts, acts that promise pleasure, give access only to terrors and an overriding impression of loss.

I sniffled and wiped my nose on the blue pillow. I had the feeling that someone was near me, that I was being watched. Had a stealthy brother seen me pissing on Hazlitt? I glanced around and saw, a few feet away, standing in a puddle, Gunner. It was only the dog. Gunner held, in his mouth, between his sharp teeth, a shoe.

"Where did you get that?" I asked. The dog padded forward. He lowered his head and dropped the shoe in a puddle.

I knelt. The shoe was a white canvas slip-on. It was not new. It might've belonged to anyone. Gunner's teeth had punctured it.

I placed my hands firmly on either side of Gunner's head. I cradled, in my hands, the dog's skull. I addressed this creature: "Listen to me. I do not want a smelly boating shoe. I want a mask. Do you remember what I told you about the Corn King? I understand that it may not make perfect sense for the Corn King to wear an *African* mask, but we don't have any other masks in our collection. This isn't the Natural History Museum, Gunner. I want you to go back and bring me a mask from the wall. They're hanging all over the wall and you'll be able to get one without much trouble. Do you think you can manage?"

Gunner licked his mouth and nose with his long pink tongue. He liked having his ears scratched. I took care not to become angry with the dog. I said, in an even, composed voice, "I have tremendous faith in you, Gunner. Much depends on the mask. Pick a good one. Use your judgment."

I released the Doberman's head. Right away Gunner picked up the deck shoe with his teeth. He turned and trotted away quickly through the darkness. He was gone and I was alone again. I did not like being alone in the stacks. I did not feel in the mood to read an old book. While waiting for Gunner's return, I examined the medicine vials in my jacket pocket. I was very pleased to find that these contained morphine. There was enough morphine here to relieve a lot of suffering. Carefully, one by one, I returned the precious vials to my jacket.

I meditated on the Corn King. It is a little-discussed fact that human sacrifices are not strictly ancient occurrences. The practice continues, among certain peoples in certain places, to draw adherents. And why not? All men experience the feelings and convictions that led the earliest savages to dread hunger, isolation, abandonment, their powerlessness against nature. These stacks, certainly, were dark and haunted by demons. I drew my coat around me and, like a little boy, a child alone, prayed to feel better. Isn't feeling better, in a general way, what blood sacrifice is for? When we draw blood from another person, either in fact or in essence, aren't we really trying to defend against our own fears, against our own desires, against loneliness?

Didn't I miss my father terribly? Didn't I love alcohol in order to know him? Didn't my brothers do the same?

I heard a noise and there was Gunner. He had an African

mask in his mouth. This mask was familiar to me. It was old, wooden and immense, a brightly painted Central African tree spirit featuring an elongated chin and pronounced, scarlet cheekbones. Horizontal knife slits served as eyes, and bushy hair fashioned from dried twigs cascaded in bunches over an expansive forehead carved from some equatorial hardwood with the peeling bark still attached.

I crouched down and the dog came to me. It was a shame, really, that I had no doggy treats along with the morphine in my pockets. I said, like a true master, "That'll do, boy." Gunner had clearly exerted himself carrying this weighty, cumbersome mask. He opened his mouth and let me extract it from between his teeth. Saliva coated it. It was not, I should say, a mask I would have selected for myself. I'd have chosen something smaller, lighter, with bigger eyes and wearing a meaner, more threatening facial expression. I would have preferred a face without bark. The bark gave an appearance of unclear skin. This mask, with its absurdly long chin and its silly hairstyle, most likely represented some friendly, comical spirit.

Any mask, even a demon's face or a Zulu war mask, will look harmless until worn by a person. If worn correctly, a mask becomes animated. The face—no matter how grotesque or exaggerated its features—seems to come alive, to change countenance, and to convey, through the gestures and movements of the wearer, the emotional spirit of the mask character. Creative animation of this sort can have a profound effect on an audience, a profounder effect on the mask's wearer. As the mask's spirit—this can be the spirit of a god, a beast, an inanimate object, or some form of vegetation—emanates *outward,* into the world, so does it penetrate *inward,* into the unconscious of the person wearing the mask. This is the mask's real purpose: to lead its wearer, gradually, by way of the ecstasy induced through physical exertion (most often a savage dancing), into a realm that is *shared by these two principal characters,* the man in the mask and the spirit symbolized by the mask. In this dark and phantasmagorical realm it is possible for the wearer to leave behind quotidian life, reconcile himself to natural forces beyond conscious understanding, and with a little luck and a few bourbons down the hatch, experience, in an instant of life, a hideous self-transformation.

I told Gunner, "When I put on this mask, I won't be myself anymore. I'll be the Corn King. But don't worry, because the Corn King will also be me. Ready, boy?"

Before I could put on the mask I had to get the rest of my costume in order. As a rule this is not difficult because my costume consists only of nakedness. Primitive, elementary, unencumbered, old-fashioned, barbaric, vulnerable, willing, childlike nakedness.

And the mask.

Tonight, however, it would be unhealthy to absolutely disrobe. The air temperature was at an all-time low. Our soaked floor would be treacherous without footwear. I elected this compromise: shoes and socks but no pants or underpants, and, for warmth, my sport jacket, but no shirt. Plus the mask. I saw no harm in carrying the pillow as a shield, a syringe for a sword.

I undressed and lowered the mask onto my head. Right away I knew that the eyeholes were going to be a problem. To see, I had to hold the mask in place by its pointed chin. This mask was incredibly heavy, and its straps—only rough twine—were frayed, inelastic, and irritating to the skin. I knotted them as tightly as I could without breaking them, then attempted a few head rotations. The mask skidded down my face and crushed my nose. There must have been ancient pollen suffusing the mask's leafy hair. Immediately I felt the urge to sneeze. And I did sneeze, not once but serially. My sneezes, which came violently, loosened the mask's straps. Again the mask slipped down and crushed my nose, and this induced another round of sneezing. I am embarrassed to admit spraying a large volume of phlegm into the mask's interior facial cavity, coating the mask's inner surface and, because I was behind the mask, my own face.

"Hang on, Gunner. These fucking things always take some getting used to."

Gunner seemed impatient, excited, eager to go. I wrestled with the mask. Suddenly I felt the Doberman's trembling, cold nose between my legs; I felt Gunner's heated breath between my naked legs, tickling my penis; and I leapt backward and cried, "Hey! Hey!"

Enough was enough. The tree spirit mask—unwieldy, gluey with mucus and the dog's saliva, improperly fastened and heavily contaminated with allergens—would have to suffice. I mashed it onto my head, yanked the straps tight, then gathered up my other Corn King paraphernalia, that blue pillow and the rapier/syringe, and said to the Doberman, "I can't see. You must lead me."

To make this happen I reached down and clutched the fur at the back of the dog's neck. I grabbed him gently because I felt a true fondness for Gunner, and also because I did not care to be attacked by this Doberman. In truth I should say that I grabbed the dog's *skin*—Dobermans are, of course, shorthairs, pretty much. Gunner set out walking, and I— sneezing, half-nude, virtually blind behind my mask, armed with ineffectual weapons, suffering one black eye and a rug-burned arm, bent over like a cripple to maintain petting contact with the dog—stumbled alongside. In this absurd and sad configuration we made our way, dog and man, through the better part of Fable and Folklore.

I made an effort, as we walked, to relax. It is important not to hyperventilate or go into cold sweats while wearing a giant headpiece. Steady breathing and a low heart rate are the keys to transformational experience.

I heard no rioting men or furniture breaking in the distance. The only noises were splashing water and our steps, Gunner's easy steps and my awkward steps, through puddles.

It was that late time of early, early morning, the lull before the new day, when a party is finishing and all the bottles have cigarettes floating in them, and only stragglers remain awake to share a drink.

Gunner and I sloshed through the aisles. The Doberman took a hard right turn and I lurched after him. "Try to find Twentieth Century," I told him. Water everywhere was rising higher—it was above my shoes, lapping around my ankles—and I whispered to Gunner, "This is some serious flooding. There must be a clogged drain somewhere."

The Doberman changed direction. He dragged me after him into a passageway that seemed, from what I could make out—which was not much with that spirit mask slipping, again and again, down my face—roomier, wider, better lit. We were almost free and I felt almost happy. I began to breathe more easily. I looked forward to the Corn King dance I would perform, and to the warming nightcap that would follow dancing. Dim light showed at the edges of my Corn King mask, and I could feel snowy wind blowing against my legs. It was only a short distance to freedom. The dog hurried to a trot.

I had forgotten all about my brothers who cruised these stacks in the late hours.

Now quite suddenly I heard men's voices around me. As we entered this broad corridor, as we passed, the dog and I, through this main aisle, I heard the low, murmuring voices of brothers I could not see, though these men were, I could tell, standing close to me.

"Look, everyone, it's the Corn King in his dark socks and his tree mask," exclaimed one voice. And another complimented, "Sweet outfit, little brother. Are you in prehistoric drag?" I realized then that I was not wearing pants. It was insane, really thoughtless, to tour our stacks without pants. I made a show of waving the hypodermic needle blindly around, but this only made me feel pathetic. These men did not want to chase me. They did not want to kill the Corn King. I was safe here. Their voices whispered. One man promised to care for me, and not to hurt me; and for a brief instant I felt a hand touching my shoulder, gently, affectionately; and I cried, "What do you want?"

No reply. I commanded the dog to walk through the crowd. Men followed behind and the red library's lights flickered ahead. Why was I so frightened of my brothers? Why so afraid of their low-pitched voices, of their touch and their acrid, peppery smells?

The dog bolted ahead and it was all I could do not to trip over Gunner and tumble into the tidal lake of melted snow and leaking water. I struggled to keep up with this animal. My feet and legs were cold and wet and numb. I splashed along, and a cheerful, younger man's voice said, as I passed, "I do like your ass, son." This sounded like Bennet talking. Should I say hello to Bennet? Would this be a reason for uncomfortableness at some later time? I couldn't resist. I said, "Bennet, how are your kids?" And the mask was sliding down and repeatedly knocking my nose, bruising my nose. The mask's straps chafed against my ears. I clutched the blue pillow and Gunner's neck as we hustled out of Literature; we limped straight out of those stacks arranged as mazes inside dusty mazes. Out we came, a lean dog guiding a battered, mostly naked man waving a syringe and wearing an enormous painted mask, out past love seats and reading lamps, past the windows with torn red curtains blowing.

My leg collided with a coffee table and I fell down and lost my grip on the dog.

I adjusted the mask, peered up, and saw, through narrow, slitty eyes, what our red library had, over the course of the long night, become.

I saw water, dripping. Dark striations marked trails where melting snow made creeping descent through the tilting walls. Plaster and wood were contaminated by runoff from our leaking slate roof.

I saw windows thrown open to the elements. The windowpanes were frosted, opaque, black, adorned with tiny icicles. The wind rushed in and debris and paper blew like damaged birds around the room until deposited on the floor.

I saw men on the floor, men curled up in chairs and laid out on couches that had been shoved clear of water that poured down in a steady stream from the brown stain.

A silent company of men huddled around the fireplace. The men stoked the flames with splintered arms and legs of furniture smashed to bits for this purpose. Bats descended from above the lights and flew their erratic patterns around the men. These brothers passed a bottle between them and I envied them. Their faces were amber, hollow, destitute in firelight. I could identify Christopher and Fielding, Tom and Milton and Donovan. Others knelt before the grate but with faces turned away.

The water cascaded down from the ceiling and splashed the rug. Shallow rivers wound beneath tables and chairs, around a dozen broken lamps, past the bodies of Maxwell, Virgil, Barry.

It was time for me to dance. It would soon be a new day. I stood up and breathed deeply in preparation. Inhale, exhale. As a rule I like to put myself through a little leg-stretching routine prior to dancing. Gentle stretching gets the blood flowing and protects against soft-tissue tears, ligament sprains, charley horses and cramps. It was going to be difficult to stretch while wearing the Corn King mask. I hopped from foot to foot, lightly, as a substitute warm-up. Normally I don't like to watch myself dance. Recognition of the body is a reminder of material existence. The dancing is an attempt to renounce the material world, surrender one's will to the mask and the unconscious, and inhabit the kingdom of the senses. Tonight, however, I broke with tradition and took a quick peek down at my stomach and my legs. My belly was not too huge but it seemed soft and what you would call *round;* as I leapt in the air, it shook in a manner I found alarming. My legs were, it seemed to me, slight; brown shoes and calf-high socks did not make them appear mighty; rather, their boniness was emphasized. Hair was rubbed away in patches. I was disappointed to notice that

my penis in the freezing air was shrunken. Often I feel
heartened by the sight of my penis. Tonight it had retreated
into me. It looked like a little boy's. I jumped up and down
and it trembled. Watching this made me feel insecure and
self-protective, and I worried about the authority I would
have over spectators. For a moment I saw myself the way
others might see me—as a soft, leaping man wearing a
weird, improvised costume: sport coat with pockets over-
flowing, a mask distinguished by its enormous complement
of leafy hair and its lengthy chin, socks and shoes but no
pants to hide genitals that did not impress. Quickly I made
this vision of myself go away. I hopped more vigorously,
breathed in and out, and little by little, began to relax. Falling water's sounds were comforting. I had the feeling that
people were watching me and so checked around to see who
was out there. Figures stirred in the shadows. A solitary
character in the vicinity of our dinner table carried a knife
that shimmered brightly. This man looked to me like Siegfried. I say this because Siegfried is thick without being fat,
and his sculptor's arms are huge. Gruff Rex was loitering
near the stone-tool collection; this unpleasant man had, it
seemed, armed himself with an ancient blade, a valuable
exhibit from our display. Both these fellows watched as I
incorporated the first flourishes into the dance, a simple
kick and gyrating, overhead arm movements, waving the
pillow and that syringe. The allergens in the mask were getting to me again and I sneezed loudly, and a voice behind
me said, "Bless you," and I turned and saw that I was

surrounded by my brothers. Drunken men converged from every side. William, Allan, Henry, Porter, and others displayed knives and sections of wood, clubs fashioned from the wrecked furniture. Seeing this, I felt that first rush of adrenaline—it was what I had been waiting for—and sped up the dance. Allan lunged at me with sharp porcelain, a lamp fragment with the contours of a rough hatchet. It was a halfhearted lunge by an aging schoolteacher and I fended Allan off with the blue pillow as Porter and Saul raised sticks and I twirled away through puddles. It was all so easy. New steps came naturally, effortlessly, and soon I was pirouetting across our waterlogged rug. When Donovan came close, I brandished the syringe, and Donovan, a known coward, backed away. Then Arthur's wooden bludgeon made contact with my shoulder. His was a good shot, but I hardly felt it. The water poured down from the ceiling and rivers snaked across the floor, past our overturned card tables with chessboards spilled and black and white armies scattered and drowning. I saw Hiram leaning on his walker inspecting teeth that were out of his mouth and shining brilliantly in his hand. Hiram scrubbed his teeth on his sleeve, and his empty mouth smiled at me as I accelerated around brothers armed with burning sticks and fireplace pokers. For sport, and to honor family tradition, I shouted a few egregious criticisms of my brothers' clothing and hairstyles. A man's body lay nearby, and I approached and peered down through the mask's eyes to see Maxwell's bloody face. Chandeliers swung and I rotated my head over Maxwell.

The sweat ran down my arms and my naked legs. This dance was a healing dance. My body felt no pain. I waved my arm and struck William hard with the pillow, whipping him with the pillow's braided tassels. Then I held the pillow and the syringe in the same hand. While Zachary and other brothers circled, grimaced, and plotted to get me, I administered painkillers to Maxwell. It took only an instant to insert the syringe's needle into a bottle from my coat's breast pocket, another instant to withdraw liquid into the transparent chamber. As I did this, I performed an elaborate dance symbolizing death, regeneration, and the spiritual childhood that follows new life. I danced ecstatically over my brother, recklessly waved the needle to intimidate Rex, Arthur, Henry, the rest; then quickly bent down, felt around for a vein, and plunged the needle into Maxwell's cold, exposed arm. "Feel better," I said to Maxwell. After that I vaulted across the rug to other brothers. I shouted at the men chasing me, "Back off if you don't want to get hurt!" I jammed Barry's stethoscope's earpieces into the mask's ears, danced from brother to fallen brother on our floor. One of these was our young Andrew and I had no clue how this man had come to be stretched out before me on the carpet, but upon closer inspection thought I observed swelling and a reddish rash around Andrew's mouth, and so drove the needle in with a full dose of lovely opiates drawn from Barry's medicine vials. I tossed syringe and bottle away, reached into my coat's pockets, took out fresh equipment. I ministered to every injured brother except dear Virgil, whose terror of needles is something I can respect even though I find it irrational and pointless. I went to man after man and emptied one bottle then the next and the next into one syringe followed by another and another. I used all the bottles and all the syringes. I was the bringer of health. I was the wearer of the stethoscope. I was the forgiving friend. I was the Corn King. I emptied syringes into men, and I was their Jesus. Water splashed down from the stain on the ceiling. The water ran over the mask and my face, and I felt cleansed and renewed. Wildly I played among the bottles and syringes littering the floor. I used my football skills to avoid Arthur and Henry diving at my feet. I heard beautiful singing in my head, and I heard wind howling and our windows rattling. I heard the cries of my brothers on the floor, and I felt the power and the peace that came from dancing. I gripped the mask by its chin and made crazy head motions. The spirit of the mask was inside me and I had no awareness of my body though I knew with exquisite understanding that human experience is made of desire. At a certain point Tom grabbed a piece of bric-a-brac from a table and threw it at my head, but this missed and crashed into the shelves. The water splashed over me and I felt happier, I believe, than I have ever felt in my life, which is to say that I felt nothing at all, not even the chill of the water or any fear of Zachary and those brothers with their blades and truncheons. My brothers moved in a circle around me. Joyfully, obliviously, peacefully, I danced with my head held back and my eyes staring upward at chandeliers. The ceiling gave up its water from a hole that opened and grew wider above my head. Bit by bit, and section by section, the wet plaster began to loosen and to crack. This was something that had been bound to happen eventually. Now it was happening. The plaster ruptured and I danced faster, spinning around and around and gazing upward at our chandeliers swinging into alignment. Shadows on our ceiling grew long, and my brothers approached closer, and I got dizzier. The terrible cracks spread across the plaster, and the first fragments of our ceiling came loose and descended and were washed away on the tide of water pouring down from Father's mouth to splash me while I danced. It was all coming together for me. Past Dougs and harvest spirits. My brothers with their knives. Ancient societies and our red library. Everything was inside me and I was one of the Martyrs. There was Father's nose. There was his horrible mustache. He stared down sadly. There was that burning cigarette, a jagged timber beam. The ceiling broke and a section of Father's forehead in profile split in two. Black fissures spread across Father's cheek, around the blood-shot eye. The water exploded from the ceiling and Father's eye burst apart and was swept away in fragments. Next the nose parted from the face and poured down in the water spitting from Father's mouth. Feature after feature came down on a waterfall. I danced in the waterfall as Father's face fell to pieces over me.

This was my undoing, really. The major section of ceiling that was the face came away from the rest of the ceiling. The dark brown water stain, eight or nine feet in diameter—this eight-or-nine-foot section of ceiling, the bulk of our father's image—detached itself in one massive portion and, loosened by leaking water, broke free, plummeted to the floor.

My brothers' voices called out. I leapt back. The plaster did not hit me. I think it might as well have hit me. The face dropped to the floor and its crash was the finale, as they say, of my little dance.

Water splashed. Chalky paste and particles like rocks flew. Dust clouds erupted into the air as Father broke apart before my feet. All the plaster shattered and a sickening compound, water and muck, covered my legs and my stomach. The muck was cold. The ceiling was ruined. I was amazed. The effect of Father's thundering, bitter crash was like that of any harsh noise or bad surprise: shock accompanied by disorientation, lasting several seconds.

That was all the time it took for my beloved brothers to advance on me, to put their hands on me, to take me from all sides and hold me so that I could not move, and to hit me with their sticks and cut me with their knives.

I turned my head away and looked over at our windows. The windows' panes were no longer black, exactly, but colored with gray, the beginnings of the morning's light.

A voice beside my ear told me to stop struggling. I felt bereaved over the ceiling's fall. My brothers ganged around me. A faraway voice shouted something and this was blind Albert alone in his chair, wanting something, rapping his cane against his horsehair chair.

Siegfried was the man in front of me and it was his knife,

I believe, that made the initial cut across my stomach. Someone else was tugging at the mask, trying to wrench the mask off, because of course the mask's elongated chin prevented the man behind me from cutting into my throat. The man behind me pressed his body against mine. I felt his legs against the backs of my legs, and I felt the man's belt buckle digging into my back. The man's arms were wrapped around me and the side of his rough face leaned against my shoulder.

"Who is that?" I asked.

"It's me. Arthur," the man answered as another brother poured a drink over the mask's painted mouth, into the mask's mouth and down over my lips. "Swallow," a voice said, and I sank to my knees on the floor.

"Spooner, is that you?" I asked the man pouring cognac over my face and mouth.

"Yes."

"Tell me what is happening," I said to my brother. I lapped at the pouring drink and the blood ran from the cut Siegfried had made with his knife across my stomach.

"They're taking off your mask," Spooner said to me. "You've knotted the strings tightly, Doug."

"I'm sorry," I said.

"We'll get it untied eventually," a voice said; and this same voice, the voice, I suppose, of the man working to remove the mask, asked, "Would someone pass me a razor?"

The jabs to my ribs hurt more than deeper wounds to my

stomach and my chest. This was true also of the sharpened table leg that I watched coming down in front of the mask, striking me on my arm.

There is an impression, held true in our society, that the father is surpassed, overtaken, outlived, and in these and other respects, killed by the son.

But this is, I think, actually not the case. In truth, I think, it is always the son who is killed by the father. Couldn't it be argued that each man dies the death made for him by his father?

I felt so terribly weary. I felt so tired, and so sleepy. It was the end of our night. I felt blessed to be held by my brothers' hands in our red library.

"I'm cold," I whispered to a man holding my hand. I could smell the man's alcoholic breath.

"Please, close the windows for Doug," this man said to others. Sure enough, a brother of mine did trudge through puddles, ice, and snow to our tall windows. I could hear the windows, one then another sliding downward. The Doberman watched from beneath the dinner table. Bats circled overhead. What in the world had become of Chuck's sheepdog? My brothers on the carpet, my brothers who had received their injections, stirred, began to move, lifted arms and legs, uttered sighs. They greeted the new day. I, on the other hand, had neither syringes nor medicines. All these things were gone.

My heart at least was beating in my chest. The mask

came off and I was Doug again and a knife was cutting me somewhere.

Before closing my eyes I gazed in the direction of our fire. It pleased me to watch our fire.

It is true that there is nothing like a blaze in the hearth to soothe the nerves and restore order to a house.